THE PIRATE WOMAN

THE PIRATE WOMAN

Captain Dingle

WILDSIDE PRESS

Originally serialized in four installments in *All-Story Weekly*
magazine from November 2, 1918, to November 23, 1918.
Published by Wildside Press LLC.
Visit us online at wildsidepress.com

CHAPTER I.

THE CAVE OF TERRIBLE THINGS.

A great unrest brooded over mountain and forest; the blue Caribbean lay hushed and glaring, as if held in leash by a power greater than that which ordered its daily ebb and flow.

Men moved or stood beneath the trees on the cliffside in attitudes of supreme awe or growing uneasiness, according to their kind: for among them were numbered Spaniard and Briton, creole and mulatto, Carib and octoroon, with coal-black negroes enough to outnumber all the rest—and it was upon these last that profound awe sat oppressively.

Apart, followed by a hundred furtive eyes, Dolores, daughter of Red Jabez, ranged back and forth before the mighty rock portals of the Cave of Terrible Things, like some magnificent tigress hedged with foes. Beyond those portals Red Jabez, Sultan of pirates, arbiter of life and death over the motley community, lay at grips with the grim specter to whom he had consigned scores far more readily than he now yielded up his own red-stained soul. Red Jabez was dying a death as hard as his lurid life had been.

Beyond those rock portals none save Jabez and Milo, the herculean Abyssinian slave, had ever passed. Dolores, next in line, was in ignorance as deep as her meanest slave, concerning what lay beyond the great mass of rock which formed the door, and which Milo alone could move. She knew, as did every one, that the great chamber of Red Jabez held some vast mystery; she suspected, as did the rest, that it concealed wealth beyond dreams; deep down in her soul she hoped that inviolate chamber held for her the means of emancipation; but of this hope, none knew save herself. For Queen of Night though the white men called her, Sultana though she was named with fear and submission by the blacks, though her power was second only to that of Red Jabez, and barely less than his, a canker gnawed at the heart of Dolores, the canker of a suspicion that her power was but a paltry power, her freedom but a caged freedom.

Somewhere beyond the great ocean thatstretched away before her eyes lay a world she knew nothing of; yet since her earliest childhood her keen mind had told her that the silk with which she was clothed, the jewels that encrusted her dagger-hilt, the ships whose pillage had yielded up these things, must come from lands far distant, more desirable than the maroon country of Jamaica. More, her ears attuned to the whisper or roar of the sea, the sigh or shriek of the winds, carried to her the mutterings of men long held in leash, who now saw in their chieftain's death the realization of their own wild dreams of riches and release. All these things told her that the great, strange world beyond the sea-line was something for her to strive for; not for the rabble who called her queen.

She paced back and forth, a splendidly lithe, glowing creature of beauty and passion, every movement a grace, each grace such as befitted a royal woman conscious of mental and physical perfection. Her hair surrounded her face and shoulders in a lustrous, rippling cloud, through which peeped a bare arm and breast stolen from the goddess of beauty; her tunic of quilted Chinese silk hung from one shoulder by a strap fashioned from the ribbon of the Star of Persia, and fastened by the star; her strong, slender waist was girdled with a heavy gold cord that supported a long, thin dagger, no toy, in a jeweled sheath; the hem of her single garment rang with gold sequins to the movement of her smoothly muscular knees; her high-arched feet were protected from thorns and shells by sandals of red leather.

As the moments passed, and no sign came from within the cave, Dolores restrained her impatience with increasing difficulty. The men scattered around were not of such stuff; they felt the impending crisis settle heavily upon them, and white and black alike drew together for the comfort of close touch. From time to time a hardier spirit uttered his thoughts aloud, yet always with a glance of uncertainty toward Dolores. They had reason to glance that way; for every man had tasted of the queen's justice, which rarely erred on the side of mildness; many of them had experienced her terrible competence to carry out a sentence in person. Of them all, not one but knew that in Dolores he owned as queen a woman who need yield nothing of prowess to any man: her knife was as swift, her round wrist as strong, her blazing violet-black eyes as sure as any among them. Not a man could ever forget the offending slave whom she had thrashed with her own hands, disdaining assistance, until the wretch tore loose and fled screaming to the cliff to pitch headlong into the shark-infested sea; nor could they forget her unhesitating dive and terrific struggle to recover him and her completion of the interrupted punishment when she had brought him back.

Yet the stress proved too great, even in face of these memories, and a tall, powerful Spaniard, heavily earringed, handsome, with a swart, brutal beauty, delivered a scorching oath to the heavy air and exclaimed fiercely:

"A curse on this babe's play! Must men stand here like whipped curs until a slave commands us enter? Come! Who'll follow me past that door? I'll know what lies behind this mummery if I choke it from old Jabez's withered neck as he dies."

The man stepped forward two paces, glaring defiantly at Dolores, waiting for men to follow. An uneasy shuffling of feet was his only answer for a moment; then his eyes shifted with cooling ardor at sight of Dolores. For a breath after he had ceased speaking, the girl stood like a splendid statue, except for the glitter of her eyes and a slight quivering of her limbs; it was as if she awaited some response; then her face relaxed into a contemptuous smile, and her crimson lips parted to reveal her even, gleaming teeth. She laughed, a rippling little laugh like the tinkle of steel links, and with a single gliding movement that permitted no avoidance she swept to within two feet of the now frightened ruffian.

"Yes? Yellow Rufe would choke words from a dying man!" she cried. "Nothing that lives and can stand on two feet is in danger from such as he. Peace, slavish dog!" she panted, flinging out a gleaming hand and seizing him by one earring. "Thus I mark curs that seek their food among the dead!" With the words Dolores's right hand flashed upward, knife-armed, and across Rufe's cheek glared a crimson cross; into his eyes leaped the fear of death.

"Now go!" she said imperiously, pushing him away. "Let no man forget that while the life is in Red Jabez he holds thy lives in pawn. When his spirit goes, ye shall reckon with me!"

Rufe staggered away, half incredulous that his punishment had fallen short of death. His companions led him apart with many a backward glance of apprehension at the authoress of his discomfiture, and a deep, sullen muttering rippled through the crowd. Dolores resumed her solitary pacing without another thought for the hardy rascal she had so swiftly and effectively softened. Her eyes were ever bent toward the great rock; her thoughts were centered on a vague, mysterious instinct which whispered to her that with her first admission into that frowning cavern the mantle of fierce old Red Jabez would fall upon her, and with it would come power that a Czar might envy! A Czar's power, indeed, but with all of a Czar's cares and more; for Czar never ruled over subjects like these.

A sudden hush fell upon the place; the mutterings ceased as if tongues were stricken stiff. Rufe, with his head now enwrapped in crossed bandages, stared toward the great rock with a wavering expression in his smoldering eyes, an expression that hovered between reluctant submission, reawakened cupidity, and dawning

7

hope. Dolores stood motionless, imperious in every line and feature, her heavy eyelashes veiling the eagerness in her eyes, her red lips curved in royal indifference.

The great rock was turning.

Slowly, yet with the flawless regularity of a millwheel, the mass of stone was rolled upward and to one side; it rested at last on a ledge, balanced perfectly, ready to fall again at the touch of a finger; and in the aperture appeared the human agent of its opening.

Milo, the giant Abyssinian, guardian of the rock, custodian of the Cave of Terrible Things, bone of contention for the jealous and terror of the strongest, filled the entrance with his colossal frame and looked out with a calm dignity that made the whites cringe with hatred. Slowly, with stately grace, the giant advanced until he stood before Dolores, and in his coal-black eyes shone the light of limitless devotion. He knelt, kissed the sequins on her tunic's hem, then, with both hands pressed to his forehead, he bowed his face to the earth at her feet.

"Rise, Milo," said Dolores, gently, and her breath caught painfully as she spoke. She knew what the slave came for; every man in that community of pirates, wreckers, escaped slaves, and convicts knew as well as she. All had awaited this moment, knowing when it came that the mystery of the cave would be a mystery no longer to at least one of them: all knew that the summons meant the passing of the old pirate who had brought them together, ruled them with blood and iron, and forced from them a homage none of them would render to his Maker.

"My Sultana, it is time," said Milo, rising and waiting. He needed to say no more.

"Lead me to my father, then," replied the girl, and stepped after the giant with sure step and resolute face, giving no heed to the renewed shuffling and congregating of her people, nor to Rufe, who again stood out before the rest and addressed them in fierce tones.

Dolores entered the great hewn-rock doorway and in spite of her stout heart and steel will she thrilled in every fiber. At the end of the frowning passage, whose ruby lamps but accentuated the gloom and imparted to it an infernal glow, lay the great chamber that only the chief might enter. What would she find there? Her father, yes, and dying! Otherwise this summons had never come. The death must be upon him now; the fierce old sea-king had held his throne-room inviolate through many bouts with the grim Reaper, knowing his own strength to conquer. But now he had called, and Dolores sought the unknown with a curiosity that beat down fear.

Behind her a heavy thud echoed along the rocky walls, and the outer light was cut off by the falling of the great stone. In a moment Milo stood beside her and, taking her hand in his, led her along the utterly invisible floor until she stood before a massive door.Her feet sank into the pile of heavy carpets; her nostrils quivered to the delicate odors of burning spices; at the top of the door a great jeweled lantern cast a rich, yellow light down the panels, and the girl gasped involuntarily at the sight revealed to her. Each panel was formed of scales that overlapped like a serpent's; the scales were roughly hammered gold and silver, richly chased, and studded thickly with gems—without any conjecture she knew them to be precious vessels that should have graced an altar, split, perhaps with a bloody cutlass, and beaten out into irregular plates to gratify some grim humor of the terrible old corsair in the long ago. Neither hinges, handle, lock, nor latch appeared on the surface; apparently the door was solidly embedded in the mighty rock itself. The giant laid a hand on the side of the door-frame, and Dolores waited with impatience for admission. For all her schooled self-control her eyes glinted with astonishment when Milo stood aside and bowed low, saying:

"Enter, my princess!"

Without a sound the massive door had vanished, sliding up and out of sight in the dark recess of the roof, leaving smooth, steel-lined slots at sides and bottom that reflected the polish of scrupulous care. Dolores stifled her surprise, and moved toward the heavy velvet hangings which still barred her way. These, too, were swept aside with no visible effort, and the girl stood on the threshold of the chamber of mystery.

CHAPTER II.

DOLORES RECEIVES HER DIADEM.

In a great canopied bed, taken from some rich looted Indiaman, Red Jabez lay motionless as an effigy in stone. His tall, powerful body was sharply outlined in coverings of silk and rare lace; the arms and crest of a ducal house were worked into the pillows that supported his massive head. His drawn, haggard face was surrounded and all but covered with a great mane of vivid red hair; his silken shirt, wide open at the neck, revealed a massive chest, whose tide of respiration had all but ceased to run. Only his eyes, fierce yet, held token of lingering life; it was as if the vital spark was concentrated into one final blaze of tremendous brilliancy.

The fierce eyes moved swiftly at Dolores's entrance, and one might have said a film of tenderness swept for an instant over the hard glint in them. It was gone as swiftly as it came, and the stare settled unwaveringly upon the stupefied girl. For stupefaction had gripped Dolores in that first entry into the great chamber. Her wildest dreams, and they had been at times fantastic, had never showed her anything measurably approaching the scene that smote her eyes now. For the moment death, Red Jabez, her destiny, everything melted into the visionary beyond and left her capable of no volition.

The great bed stood in the center of a vast cavern; sides, roof, floor, every inch of the rock itself bore proof of the handiwork of hundreds of cunning craftsmen; but the furnishings filled Dolores's eyes to the exclusion of all else. Divans and chairs, cabinets and tables carried the mind far away to the realm of emperors and kings; vases from China and Greece stood on stands of boule-work; a tall ebony-and-ivory clock-case, in which ticked sonorously a masterpiece of Peter Hele, stood between two gorgeous pieces of Gobelin tapestry. And around her and above, Dolores's amazed eyes lighted upon gems of the painter's art such as few collections might boast. The entire ceiling was covered with a colossal "Battle of the Amazons," by Rubens, each figure thrown out in startling distinctness, full of voluptuous life and action; the walls were mantled by vast golden frames holding the best of Titian, Correggio and Giorgione, Raphael and Ribera. And jewels flashed everywhere; cunningly placed lamps, themselves encrusted with the reddest of rubies, the subtlest of green emeralds, flooded walls and furnishings with a soft yet searching light which seemed to be carefully calculated to accentuate those things whose beauty demanded light, yet to leave the eye unwearied.

"The hour has struck, my Sultana," said Milo anxiously, and Dolores shook off the spell and approached the great bed. Red Jabez closed his eyes as she leaned over him, and his lips now alone gave evidence of life. The girl, reared among the wildest of desolate isolation, knowing no softening ties of family, her impulses and emotions those of a beautiful animal, and increasingly so because of her station among the rabble that called the dying man chief, stared down at her terrible parent without a trace of visible regret: rather in her eyes shone the triumph of a victor about to enter upon a conquered kingdom. But the red pirate was speaking, and she bent her ear to catch his words. It required no physician's knowledge to perceive in his damp face all the signs of imminent dissolution.

"Dolores, my traverse is run," whispered Jabez. The effort all but stole his breath. He paused; then summoning all the tremendous will that had dominated his frame when surging with strength, he told what he had to say in short sentences, nursing the flickering spark to force his speech. "Never leave here, girl. Let no man go, either. The world has forgotten me and all of us; but memory is tenacious—it will revive at a hint; every throat that pulses with hot life here—yes, my daughter, even your fair throat—was measured years ago—a rope awaits every one. But here—"

"Yes, father?" Dolores shivered in the pause; the silence chilled her. The giant Abyssinian stood at the head of the bed, and now moistened the dying lips with wine. Red Jabez strained convulsively, snatching at his throat, and resumed with weaker voice.

"Here I have been king; here you are queen; all these things you see, and many more, are yours; life and death are in your hands to give or withhold. Keep the steel hand, though you wear the glove, Dolores. You have learned power; with the greater power you take from this chamber, and with Milo, let nothing, no man, stir your fears. Keep this chamber as I have kept it; it is your strength; when danger threatens to beat you down, here you will find—"

The fluttering whisper ceased. The old pirate lay rigid. Dolores, having heard so much, yet so little, hovered over the bed in an ecstasy of unsatisfied hunger for more; Milo stood by, a magnificent statue in living bronze, his eyes set in a steady blaze on the face of his master. Once more the blue lips moved. Dolores darted

11

down with eager ear, her hands clasped as if in supplication.

"Milo—tell," came the whisper, and with it went up the soul of Red Jabez to face a tribunal more dread than any earthly judge his body had eluded. And the tall clock ticked his knell.

Dolores flung herself down on the bed, patting the dead face with nervous fingers; but she was dry-eyed, no filial despair raised tumult in her breast, her pleading was for the impossible—for the dead lips to speak—and when she was refused her plea, she sprang from the couch in a paroxysm of royal fury:

"Now, by the powers of evil, he shall lie uncoffined until those secretive lips read me the riddle they have half told!" she cried, pacing between bed and wall with uplifted arms and hard, glittering eyes. She suddenly paused in her wild walk, turned swiftly, and reached the bedside with the same subtle, gliding sweep that had carried her before Yellow Rufe; it was a characteristic movement with her—a compound of the gliding dart of the tiger-shark and the silent-footed pounce of its jungle brother. Milo roused from his dejection and sprang from his knees with amazing promptitude, but he had yet to round the bed-foot when the splendid fury stood panting over the corpse.

"Speak!" she cried, shaking the coverlet savagely. Milo, with horror in his shining face, gently removed her hand, then stood before her with bowed head, his cavernous chest heaving wildly.

"Fool! Leave me!" she snapped, and struck the slave with all her savage force on the cheek. Milo's face turned gray for a flashing instant, then the doglike devotion that filled his heart shone through his eyes, and he knelt at the furious girl's feet, his head to the ground. In a moment he stood up and, laying a hand reverently upon Dolores's shaking shoulders, he gazed deep into her eyes. She shivered again at the uncanny hint of volcanic might effused by the giant—volcanic, yet quiescent for the moment. His lips opened to speak; and shesprang to the reaction. Now a fresh fury seized her at the slave's temerity; she flung off his hand, and snatched forth her dagger.

"Strike, Sultana," said Milo simply. He drew aside the strap of his leathern tunic, baring his heart. "Strike, but first suffer thy slave to release thee from this tomb."

"Release? Tomb? What talk is this?" gasped Dolores, her dagger held poised aloft, her lips quivering.

"A tomb it is if thy servant falls, Sultana. None save I can open the great door. Close it? Yes, any might close it. Come, I will lead thee out of this awful presence; then at the gate thou shalt send Milo to his master who loved him."

12

Slowly Dolores slipped her dagger into the sheath, and her face was bowed in confusion. All her life, the giant slave had tended her, guarded her steps and her sleep, taught her the exercises that had made her feared by all the turbulent crew outside; and she was now permitted the saving grace of remembrance. She gave him her hand, and allowed him to place it upon his head, always his favorite means of expression when she followed an outburst of rage with contrition; and in softer tone she begged for an answer to the riddle that had been left with her.

"Come, Sultana," Milo said, once more laying a hand on her shoulder, this time without resentment from her. "Thy father, the Red Chief, left much to be told; I will tell thee all, but not now. Patience, princess," he pleaded, catching the warning glint in her eyes, "dost thou hear nothing? Listen attentively—no, not in here, outside—bend thy ear to this tapestry; 'tis before a cunning sounding stone through which voices may well be heard on the cliffside. Listen."

Dolores listened with bad grace, for she regarded this as a subterfuge of the giant's, and resentment was very ready to rise in her again. But in a moment her indifference vanished; she grew alert; her body tensed, and her limbs quivered; the glitter of a queen in righteous anger lighted her eyes, and she raised an unnecessary hand to impress silence upon the slave.

"Hast hear this before now?" she demanded in a vibrant whisper.

"Since thou entered, Sultana. It could be nothing but rebellion; yet was I loath to burden my chief with this trouble in his hour of passage. But I know now that it has risen to heights which demand swift action; therefore I have made thee aware of it."

"'Tis that villain Rufe again!" muttered Dolores, still pressing her ear against the tapestry. The murmur of a hundred voices came clearly to her, and above all sounded the high-raised shout of one who harangued the rest. At periods the murmuring became a howl, and the triumphant note in it left scant room for doubt as to the nature of the address. The girl, faced with the responsibility of decided action, no longer able to depend on the wisdom and terrible power of Red Jabez, stepped from the wall with panting heart and parted lips, but with no trace of fear. Uncertainty moved her; uncertainty as to the resources of the great chamber, whose mysteries had scarcely begun to unfold for her ere the curtain was dropped again. Her stout spirit decided for her.

"Come, lead me out, Milo," she ordered, drawing herself royally erect and slipping her dagger around nearer her hand. "We must cool that rabble before the fire spreads further. Take a weapon, open the door, and follow me."

"It is the decision of a fit daughter of my chief," replied Milo, his great frame

13

expanding to the bounding energy that surged through him. Unknown to her, his eyes had never left Dolores while she was making her decision; now joy and ardor suffused and transfigured him. Slave he was, yet it was he who looked the royal part in that instant.

"Wait but a breath," he said, and reached in two gigantic strides a massive oaken chest heavily fastened with wrought iron. Lifting the lid with reverence, he took out a plain gold circlet and returned to Dolores.

"Thy father bade me make this and keep it until thou wast my Sultana, indeed," he said. He raised the heavy, dull-gold band, and placed it upon Dolores's brow with the courtly homage of a born noble. It fitted to perfection—as indeed it should, since theloving fingers that had fashioned it had crept around the girl's sleeping head many times to that end—and feminine vanity would not permit Dolores to ignore the fit. She stepped over to a long gilt-framed mirror, and her beautiful face grew dark and her violet eyes dusky at the glorious reflection that gazed out at her.

"It is well, Milo; I thank thee," she smiled. "Now to scatter the rats that gnaw at my walls. Lead out quickly."

Milo entered the passage, raising the plated door and letting it fall after them. He disdained to carry a weapon; but Dolores was content, for she had witnessed what those huge hands could do. As they approached the great stone at the entrance, the sounds outside rang through the corridor, and the sharp reverberations that accompanied them at intervals told of an assault on the rock itself with pikes, crowbars, or other smaller rocks. Milo stooped to the sill of the rock, and placed his hands beneath it.

"Stand away," he whispered, and strained his arms. "Let thy servant go out and silence this clamor—"

"Open quickly!" she interrupted him, imperiously. "It is not for the slave to precede the sovereign. Peace, and open."

Her hand was on her dagger, her head was raised proudly; every inch and line of her figure irradiated splendid strength and surety; Milo heaved at the rock, and smiled blissfully. This was indeed how he had dreamed of his Sultana when she should come into her own.

He heaved steadily, and the great rock rose from one side, rolling up and up until it balanced on the ledge; but Milo knew there was some agency at work that hindered the raising of it; never before had it been a task to bring sweat to his brow, and now he dripped from every pore. The rock refused to balance without his hand upon it, and he dared not take his shoulder away to look over the top lest it fall and crush him. He cast an appealing look toward Dolores, who was impatiently waiting for him to stand clear, and she stepped past him to the outside. She was greeted with a roar of derision that echoed far down to the sea.

"Peace, dogs of the devil!" she cried with one hand upraised. A roaring guffaw answered her. Then a burly ruffian, one-eyed and marked by a great cutlas-scar that ran from his chin across his broken nose and ended somewhere among the roots of his hair, stepped forward with a smirk of confidence, and made a mock curtsy.

"Queen o' the pirates, we salute ye!" he said. Then threw away all pretense, and swore a ripping curse to the destination of his soul. "Come, my girl," he shouted, "the game's played to a finish. Th' old buck is dead, an' we want some o' them pretties he hid away inside. You're a nice gal, I don't deny, and we ain't going to harm ye if ye don't hinder us; but we ain't playin' kings an' queens no more. Come now, let the big feller take us in, and say no more about it, for have our fling, we will."

The mob had edged nearer, until now they surged around the entrance so close to Dolores that she felt the breath of the leaders. She noticed with sharp wonderment that Yellow Rufe was not among the foremost; but she was given no time to surmise, for the mob pressed on until she was forced either to risk an advance or give ground. A little shock rippled through her when she turned swiftly to see how Milo fared, and found him gone. The mob saw it, too, and seethed about her with hungry faces.

"Come on, lads!" they howled. "Milo's gone inside to open up the loot for us." A grimy hand snatched at the girl's tunic, and in a flash the entrance was choked with fiercely striving shapes.

With a gasping cry of fury Dolores struck aside the bold hand, and with a panther-spring she was upon him. One slender, brown hand, strong as a steel claw, gripped his throat; the other hand gripped a glittering dagger that swept like the arrow of fate to his heart and dropped him a log at her feet. Just for a breath the crowd paused in awe; then hoarsely growling they packed forward again, and Dolores found herself fighting desperately against men maddened into steel-armed wolves, thirsty for her blood in payment for that split. She more than held her own by sheer skill and suppleness for a space; but assailed from all sides save the back she speedily felt her limbs growing heavy and awkward, and a cutlas sang above her bent head when her foot had failed, leaving her without guard or avoidance.

Then she knew that she had been permitted to win her spurs. For the threatening cutlas was caught in mid air by a huge bare hand, wrenched from its owner's grasp, and returned point first into the assailant's breast. And Milo's deep voice rang in her ear:

15

"Step into the passage, Sultana, and swiftly. Have a care for the body on the floor, but tarry not. To pause is to die!"

She felt herself drawn inside, the battle seemed to leave her isolated, the passage was as still as a cloister after the turmoil outside, and she stumbled along in the dim red glow, barely avoiding tripping over a body on the floor which a glance showed her to be a corpse. This was the man who had tried to crush back the rock door on Milo.

Dolores spurned the body with her foot, and abruptly turned back, in a rage to think that she had permitted the giant slave to order her into skulking security. She halted as swiftly as she had turned; for in the aperture at the end of the passage the huge form of Milo stood, both hands raised, and in them a cask was poised. A queer, spluttering sound at first puzzled Dolores; then she made out a short, hanging fuse depending from the cask, and it spluttered as it dwindled, flinging sparks around the giant's bowed head until the point of fire seemed ready to disappear in the bung-hole.

"Treasure for dogs!" roared Milo. "Divide it among thee!" The great rock thudded down as the cask hurtled out into the mob; the next instant the cavern shook and quivered to a terrific explosion; a moment after the earth might have been dead for all sound in the passage; yet another moment and the outer world rang with cries and shrieks, curses and entreaties, and Milo bowed low to his mistress and said:

"Now if my Sultana deems fit, it is time to show this scum of the earth their sovereign."

"Wait, Milo," replied Dolores, shuddering slightly at sight of him. The giant was streaked and splashed with blood; for in those moments when he stood defenseless before casting his infernal machine, a dozen cutlases and knives had sought his life.

"Pardon thy slave," he returned, sensing her meaning. "I will go thus. 'Twere not good that these dogs should know their wounds can hurt. Such scratches are nothing. They are paid for in full."

"It is well. Lead out again, good Milo, and fear not for me. With thou beside me I am armed in proof."

Again they emerged into the air, but now a deathly silence received them. Silence broken only by the rustling of garments, as a withered old crone shambled forward and cast herself at Dolores's feet.

16

CHAPTER III.

THE GROVE OF MYSTERY.

Dolores stood still, sweeping the scene of destruction with a gaze of flinty penetration. The groveling crone at her feet affected her like something unclean, and she spurned the old woman with her foot, stepping aside with a gesture of disgust. Then she raised her right hand, and cried with bitter scorn:

"Come, my brave jackals! Come to the feast prepared for thee." She lowered her hand and with a contemptuous smile indicated the gruesome results of the explosion of Milo's awful bomb.

On the edge of the forest the hardier rascals had halted; at her word they glared loweringly at her and the impassive giant at her back; from the shadow of the trees yellow and brown and black faces peered in quivering terror; but none responded to her command to approach her. The old woman on the ground alone made audible reply, and her slavish whining enraged Dolores. With a stamp of her sandaled foot she tore from her waist the gold cord, slipped off the dagger sheath, and fell upon the wretched old servitor with a shower of blows.

"Silence, old cat!" she cried, and the blows fell heavily. "Up with thee, and away. Go quickly, and make ready thealtar in the Grove of Mystery. Cease thy bleating, old witch, and summon thy shaky wits against the ordeal I shall put thee to. Some one among ye stirred up the rising which resulted as ye now see. That one I shall know before sundown, and he shall bitterly repent him. Away!"

Dolores was astonished at seeing no sign of Rufe, but outwardly she showed none of her astonishment. A more vital consideration was present in the disobedience of the motley crew who as yet made no effort to come to her call. Drawing herself fully erect when the old woman departed, she again stretched out her hand and cried:

"Dogs of Satan! I await your homage. Red Jabez lies dead: yet his spirit lives in me, your queen. By so many breaths that ye flout me, by just so many torments shall I have ye torn. Come, dogs. Kneel!"

17

A hoarse murmur went up from the forest edge, and first one by one, then in knots of half a score each, the negroes and half-breeds slunk into the open and approached her with eyes full of panic. The whites, not so susceptible to abstract influence, still hesitated, drawing near to each other in growling consultation. Dolores gave them no sign, though she watched them keenly from under her lowered lashes. She gave her attention to the line of abject creatures who filed slowly past her, each one stopping to grovel in the dust at her feet and passing on. These Milo halted near by and herded into a shivering, frightened mob. And Dolores's cool disregard of the whites had its calculated effect. One by one they stepped out into the open as had the colored men; the more timorous, or superstitious, came first, some wearing shamed grins, others palpably impressed by the example of the others and shuffling on their way uncomfortably. Last of all came the bolder spirits, and these wore faces intended to express contempt, or at least sarcastic indifference; but the faces changed invariably on closer approach to the queen. Memory proved a stubborn master; in every man's breast remembrance clamored to them to have a care how they bore themselves before this beautiful fury they called queen.

Still Yellow Rufe came not.

When all had knelt, and all had been herded by the giant Milo in two separate parties, the number was tallied, and of the whites, besides Rufe, seven were missing. One lay inside the passage; of the rest there were remains lying about the rocky wall to the cavern that might be three men or six—human discernment could never decide which.

Dolores faced her mongrel subjects again and her dark eyes blazed with fire, her beautiful face was dark with surging blood, every line of her lithe figure quivered as she spoke:

"I seek the dog who stirred ye up to mutiny!" she cried. "Yellow Rufe, if it be he, is not among ye, nor is he one of these carrion scattered on the ground. If it be some other villain, him I will know before the sun has stretched my shadow to the cliff. Deliver him up to me, and he alone shall repay. Disobey, and every biting dog among ye shall swiftly learn the price of disobedience. I wait."

The sun was fast setting, and already the shadows had grown long. Five minutes at most would see the shadow of Dolores's head at the base of the great rock, and the blacks started whimpering with apprehension. Among the whites a tremendous quiet reigned; but sullen brows here, snarling teeth there, gave hint of their interest in the sun's progress. Still no man spoke. Rather they looked at each other questioningly as the minutes flew, as if the culprit were indeed not among them.

But Dolores was wise beyond her years, wise with a wisdom bred of her volcanic existence in such a station, and she refused to be hoodwinked by the apparent absence of the man she sought. Her shadow touched the rock, and without another second of hesitation she turned toward the forest fringe, walking with majestic carriage and looking neither to right nor left. She simply uttered one short sentence: "To the Grove!"

Every man with dark blood in his veins followed her like a sheep, for terrible things had been witnessed in the Grove of Mysteries: things far beyond the understanding of such men. The sullen whites hung backagain, for their colder blood was not impregnated with the fears and superstitions that exerted such tremendous sway over their colored fellows. Still Dolores gave them never a look; she walked on, and the forest closed behind her, as if she believed her footsteps followed by every foot in the unruly crew.

It was Milo who constituted her dependable rearguard. Milo was there, and Milo would see to it that no skulker declined his queen's command. There lay the reason why Dolores so placidly turned her back to men whose dearest ambition would have been realized by the plunge of steel between her shoulders at that moment. Milo walked around to the rear of the hesitant mob, and without a word gripped the hindmost in his two great hands and hurled him bodily over the heads of his mates in the desired direction.

"Swine!" swore a harelipped Mexican, whipping out his cutlas. "I'll see your black heart for that!" and furiously made play to avenge insult to his sorely handled fellow.

The black giant turned as calmly as if his mistress had called him, and seized the fellow's cutlas hand in one huge fist, crushing bone and steel into gory pulp without visible effort. His lips never opened, his tremendous chest was ruffled not one whit; Milo's eyes alone gave warning of what he might do if occasion arose; and fooled by his obvious carelessness, the white men closed around him, knives and cutlases drawn, frantic for his life.

They should have known better. Their lessons had been many and vivid; but not a man of them all was of the caliber to learn from a slave. Milo kept hold of his man's hand, and at the scrape of steel leaving scabbard, he brought up his free hand and grasped the fellow's left wrist. Then, springing aside with the resistless impulse of a charging buffalo, he gained a clear space, and began to swing his victim by the wrists.

One complete circle was made with the human club, then a catlike ruffian watched his chance and darted in with murderous knife at Milo's breast while the dreadful club was at his back. Cool as a mountain spring, the giant immediately let

19

go his man, letting him fly far behind him like a stone from a catapult. In a twin-kling of an eye, the great hands that released the one captive closed afresh on the new assailant in front, and now the giant gave no further grace. His fingers tight-ened on the man's throat and the desperate face went black. Then, keeping the fel-low ever before him, he suddenly flung him into the air by the waist, shifting holds with tigerish swiftness, and caught him by the ankles as he came down. He whirled the unfortunate wretch once, and three men went down under the terrible blow; the rest scattered with furious howls, bespattered with the blood of their comrade; but one more sight of the unruffled giant cowed them; none attempted further knife or sword-play. Then Milo smiled scornfully, and uttered: "Go!" and they went to the forest like jackals before the lion. The giant saw them on their way, and tossing his fearful weapon over the cliff, strode after them, an awful embodiment of relentless, all but limitless strength.

The forest lay hushed and dim beyond the fringe; whispering leaves and crack-ling twigs sounded sharp as a shower of stones in the stillness. Great trees reared their majestic heads to mingle their foliage and shut out the light; every creeping, flying, walking creature seemed awed into a vague murmuring that was deeper than silence. The Grove of Mysteries was a semicircular space of cool, mossy sward, bowered in great trees and tangled vine screens; its background was the bare rock of the cliffside itself—actually, though unknown to the rabble, the outer rocky wall of the great chamber—and against this stood the altar.

The old woman had made use of her skinny limbs to good effect, impelled by a fear that had become terror. The altar was resplendent in silk and velvet, fashioned for an altar very different from this; but in place of the vessels usually associated with so sacred a piece of furniture, the Altar of the Grove was embellished with a mosaic of skulls and bones surrounding a complete skeleton which held its head in one grisly hand.

In the hollow eye-sockets glowed a weird fire that darted forth at irregular inter-vals like glances of demoniacal hate; at the altar foot a great censer erupted a dense cloud of pungent smoke that rendered the altar and those about it still more vague and ghostly. And the glade was full of cowering, slavering blacks and half-breeds, whose superstitious terrors reached high tide with each succeeding swirl of smoke or outflash of eye-socket fires.

Dolores went directly to the old woman, who stood in cringing subservience with a plain white garment in her hands. This she placed on the girl's shoulders, fastening it at the bosom with a small skull of jade stone whose grinning teeth were pearls, and whose eye-sockets were empty with an awful blackness. The gold circlet was discarded, and in its place Dolores placed on her head a turban formed from a stuffed coiled snake, whose neck and head darted hither and thither on cunning springs with her every motion and gesture.

To this awesome place came the herd that Milo drove before him; and not a man among the hardened crew was hardy enough to carry his bravado into the Grove. Blacks and whites alike, no matter what their inmost thoughts might be, yielded to the spell of the place the moment their feet trod the sward and the congregation settled into the places allotted to them.

Dolores glided out in front of the altar, and eyes glittered, dusky throats went constricted and dry with terror when she stirred up the brazier and was hidden for a moment in the rising volume of blue smoke in which flashes of devilish light played incessantly. Milo stepped up behind and above the altar, and as the smoke reeked about him vanished seemingly into the face of the cliff. There, in an unsuspected outlet to the great chamber, was the key to much of the magic with which Dolores kept her turbulent crew on the borderline of fear. She flashed a glance holding much of anxiety after her giant servitor, and busied herself about the altar to gain time.

She had received from his hands as he stepped up the effigy of a man in black wax, and now she advanced with hand upraised for silence. It was unnecessary: the silence of the dead prevailed in the Grove. With the image held aloft Dolores was a magnet that drew all eyes inevitably. Six inches tall, the image was a cleverly modeled composite of every type in the motley band; and every man realized this. Placing the effigy on the altar, Dolores seized from the brazier a glowing coal with her bare hands and placed it behind the figure. Then she flung both hands high and her vibrant voice pealed through the Grove.

"Regard all men the voice of the gods! By this sacred fire shall this image be melted; and when it is gone, out of its many likenesses shall remain the shape of him who stirred ye to mutiny against me. That shape I shall show ye by the power of my will. Lest ye disbelieve that I have this power, behold! Look for proof in the smoke behind me!"

As she spoke she stirred the incense to a dense cloud of smoke, and her blazing eyes, turned from her people, peered through the reek for a reassuring sign from the rock, for what she now demanded of Milo called for superhuman swiftness and surety. As the seconds sped, she kept the smoke swirling thickly, and her voice rang out in a weird incantation that kept the spectators trembling with the growing suspense.

Then a triumphant note entered her speech; the smoke rose thicker for an instant, then dissolved; and as it vanished, high on the rocky cliff, framed, as it seemed, in the solid rock itself, stood the grim, cold figure of the dead Red Jabez.

In this, her grave extremity, Milo the strong, Milo the slave, more than all, Milo the faithful, had not failed her.

CHAPTER IV.

THE PIRATES' BARBECUE.

A moment of ghastly hush prevailed, then the Grove shook from sward to tree-tops—pandemonium broke loose and all were in turmoil.

No need now to wait for the verdict of the wax image; no further shifting of brazen glances, or winking of knowing eyes. Shrill voices of terrified blacks, hoarse bellowings of the hardiest rascals who had ever kissed a dripping cutlas, the throaty roar of men who had played willing lieutenants to the ringleader: all pealed up to high heaven for the culprit to come forth and taste of the queen's justice rather than wait for her vengeance.

"Rufe! Yellow Rufe!" they howled. They howled it until the forest echoed with the word.

"Peace, Devilspawn!" cried Dolores, covering the crowd with an all-embracing smile of utter scorn. "Think ye I need to hear the name? Go, all of ye! Fill your swinish skins with liquor, and trouble me no more this day. When I will that Yellow Rufe appear, here he shall be drawn, whether he will or not. And in your carousal let this thought be with ye: Ye are dogs and slaves of dogs; by my will ye live, at my word ye die. The Red Chief is dead; I am your law, your queen, owner of your bodies and souls! Let any of ye seek to imitate Yellow Rufe, and Milo shall pick your limbs apart as if ye were flies. Go now; there is rum broached, and wine; make a barbecue, and fill yourselves to bursting like the vultures ye are!"

"Hello, lads, that's your sort!" roared a purple-faced ruffian with a hang-lip. "A right proper gal is that. Give her a huzza and crack yer pipes, lads!"

"Bravo, Hanglip!" bellowed another of the same kidney. Spotted Dog had lost part of an ear, and the same knife had seamed his flabby jowl into the likeness of a bloodhound's cheek; his deeply-pitted visage completed the ensemble, and no other name would have fitted him as well. "Bravo, old cutthroat! Let her play queens an' fairies, if she wants to. Here's for th' jolly grog, lads. Hey, Stumpy, start a cheer for th' pretty wench!"

So had the spell of the Grove left them immediately they smelled the fleshpots. But Dolores still held the altar; and Stumpy, having a keener memory perhaps than most of his fellows, took the warning that flashed from her angry eyes. He shivered slightly as his gaze met hers, then, hopping forward on his one good leg and club-foot, he swung a knotty fist against Spotted Dog's creased jowl and growled:

"A turn wi' that poison tongue, Spotted Dog. All hands, too, hear me talkin'. Here's a royal feast spread for us, an' th' spreader's queen o' th' pirates! Don't ever ferget that, lads. I ain't hankerin' fer what Rufe'll get. Away wi' you, now, an' I'll slit th' winepipe o' th' dog as says disrespect to th' queen."

And so the rascals trooped down to their hut-village. Noisily, profanely, full of horseplay and ear-burning jests; but never a voice spoke any word that failed in its homage when Dolores was the theme.

Snugly settled around the great rock door, the pirates' village looked out from a broad level platform over the darkening evening sea. In the center, its rear abutting on the rock itself, stood the great council hall and the dwelling of Dolores. In front of this black slaves busily heaped a great bonfire; torches were thrust into iron rings on doorpost and tree-trunk; noisy ruffians tramped into a cool cave in the rock and trundled forth casks and horn cups; while Sancho, the Spaniard, bent over a whet-stone, giving his knife a final edge against the arrival of the meat.

A venomous devil was this Sancho, and his contorted face, with the missing eye covered by a black patch, worked demoniacally in the gathering darkness with each leaping flame of the ignited torches. The hand that clutched the knife was a thing of horror; two fingers and half the thumb remained from some drunken brawl to serve the Spaniard in future play for work or debauch; and the man, crouching low over his stone, made a picture of incarnate hate that had no humor in it.

"Where's th' flesh?" screamed Sancho, looking up, his mutilated thumb running creepily along the knife-edge.

"Whet your tusks, lads, here's the blessed manna!" squealed Caliban, a hunch-backed terror, who kept his maimed carcass secure by virtue of his viperish temper, coupled with an uncanny skill of the cutlas. "Milo's our man! Huzza for Milo!"

Out from the trees stalked the giant Abyssinian, and the shadows and torchlight distorted him to grotesque proportions. He walked as if his weight was nothing; yet on his great shoulders he bore a half-grownox, its feet hobbled, its tongue hanging from its panting mouth. Straight to the fire he stepped and cast his burden down, turning again without a word and going back to the rock portals.

"Meat for men!" screamed Sancho, crouching again, knife in hand.

"For men!" echoed Caliban ferociously, and whipped his cutlas out. "Stand

24

clear!" he howled, and Sancho dodged aside. The little terror's blade sang through the air with a wicked whistle; it curved high over Sancho, then flashed down and plunged through the throat of the ox, pinning the beast to the earth. And when he recovered his breath the Spaniard swooped upon the prize, and his knife completed what the dwarf had well begun.

Then began an orgy that must render description bald and colorless. Casks were broached by knocking out the heads; long horns of cattle were filled to slopping over with rare wine or powerful rum; and then up leaped Hanglip on to an un-broached cask, cup in hand, and bellowed a toast that set the trees, the sea, the skies clamoring with rasping applause.

"The next vessel as heaves in sight, lads! May her sails be silk, her masts be gold, and her great cabin full o' rum, with a pretty wench sittin' atop o' every keg!"

From the fire came the odor of roasting meat, and the black night came down outside, making of the small circle where the pirates sprawled a blotch of infernal light, peopled with infernal shapes. But a sprinkling of faces a shade less evil leav-ened the mass; for to the feast came trooping the women of the camp: of a kidney with the men—yet women, with women's beguilements and softnesses.

Dolores sat alone in the great chamber, careless of the noise outside, her beau-tiful face dark with somber passion. Beside her chair Milo had placed her treasure chests; hers now, through the death of the terrible old corsair who had amassed them. Idly she had heaped the table with a glittering collection of gems that an em-press might well have found interest in; but Dolores frowned as at so much dross, for her thoughts were far away. The filmiest of lace and silken shawls, jeweled slip-pers, gossamer-gold head dresses, pearls and rubies from India and Persia—all lay in confusion at her hand, and aroused no spark of joy in her breast. From time to time her brooding eyes flashed and fastened upon a priceless Rembrandt "Laugh-ing Cavalier" on the wall opposite; they flashed again when her gaze shifted to a colossal Rubens "Rape of the Sabines"; her face lighted for an instant when her fingers in groping closed upon a cobwebby golden net, scintillating with cunningly wrought jeweled insects caught in the meshes, which had once graced the all-pow-erful head of Pompadour.

"Where such things are, are better!" she whispered vehemently, clenching her strong, slender hands fiercely. "Where such are fashioned and worn there are peo-ple worthy my power. My people! Pah!" she burst out passionately. "My people? Dogs! Cattle! Brutes without souls! There—" she flung a hand impetuously to-ward the "Laughing Cavalier"—"there is the pirate who should call me queen! There"—with a gesture toward Rubens's great canvas—"are men that I would com-

25

mand. Here, I must stay, why? Because a dead man willed it so. May I wither eternally if I make not my own laws. Milo!"

She clapped her hands, and in a moment the giant was before her, reverent awe in every line of his huge body.

"Sultana?"

"Are my beasts well fed?"

"They eat like crocodiles, guzzle like swine, Sultana."

"See that the liquor flows freely, Milo. And a word in thy ear. We shall go from here as quickly as the fates will send a ship. Let no sail pass henceforth."

"Lady, that may not be—"

"Silence! Give me no may not! When I, Dolores, will to go, who shall stay me?"

"Death lies beyond the horizon for thee as for all of us, Sultana. Pirate the Red Chief was last of the band; every man who calls thee queen is under sentence of death; the pillage of a hundred ships lies here. Here is safety. The Red Chief's law—"

"Peace! I am the law! Seek me that ship—and quickly. Shall I live among such carrion, when the world is peopled withsuch as those?" she cried with a sweeping gesture toward a life-size "Three Graces," by Correggio, epitomizing feminine grace indeed.

"Thou art fairer, Sultana," replied the giant simply; and the girl flushed warmly for all her moody dissatisfaction. She smiled kindly upon the slave, and said more softly: "Thy devotion pleases me, Milo. Yet is my will unchanged. Seek me that ship. I will go from here. Stay, if thou wilt, or art afraid."

"Lady," returned the giant, "when the Red Chief, thy father, took me from the slave ship he gave me liberty—liberty to serve him. He has gone; my care is now the queen, his daughter. Going or staying, Milo remains thy bodyguard. Pardon if I offended thee; thy father desired what I have told thee. But the ship. This evening, at sundown, a sail leaped in sight beyond the Tongue."

"This evening! And ye said no word of it?" cried Dolores, blazing with fresh anger. She leaned forward in her chair as if crouching for a spring.

"It passed as swiftly as it appeared, Sultana. No other eye save mine saw it; the men know nothing—"

"It is well, Milo. I had forgotten thy eyes were twice as keen as any other man's. Keep that condor's vision of thine bent to seaward, and tell no man of what comes into view. Bring me the news; I shall know how to keep my rascals in hand. Now go and send to me a woman to serve me: a young woman, nimble and deft; give the

26

old woman to the cooks for scullery drudge."

"A woman here, Sultana?"

"Here! What bee buzzes in thy great head now?" The giant again looked grave; the girl's impatience surged anew.

"Sultana, don't forget that, save thee and me, servant of the great chamber, none may enter here and go alive?"

"Now by the fiend, enough!" blazed the girl. "Again, I am the law! Wilt have it imprinted on thy great body with my whip?"

Milo made a low obeisance, departed without further speech, and in a few moments ushered in from the bacchanalian revels a maid for his mistress.

"Pascherette will serve thee well, Sultana," he said, leading the girl forward. He saw approval in Dolores's face and departed, his luminous black eyes unwontedly soft and limpid.

CHAPTER V.

MILO SIGHTS A SAIL.

Day broke through a silver haze, and as the blue sea unrolled to view, far down to the southeast, flashed a pearly sliver of sail lazily drawing in to the coast. It was the merest streak of white against the sky, and none but Milo's sharp eyes could have seen it. Even at that distance, and indistinct though it was in the mist, the giant detected the three masts crossed with yards that proclaimed the vessel a full-rigged ship. He gazed long and earnestly, to assure himself of the ship's progress, then hurried along the mountain toward the village.

He strode with the free stride of a perfect creature, swinging from the hip and covering the ground at a common man's running pace. His vast chest heaved and fell easily and rhythmically, the golden-hued skin rippling and flashing in the rising sunlight; every line of limbs and torso was the outward and visible sign of abounding health; the straight black hair falling to his shoulders framed a keen, powerful face of Semitic mold, in which the high brow and calm, fearless eyes belonged rather to one of the blood-royal than to a slave. And rightly, too, for Milo, the giant, was of princely line in his own land, and his present servitude was an accident that had yet failed to rob him of his birthright of dignity.

He came abreast of and above the haven where lay the stout sloop and boats of the community, and the sounds of noisy industry about the craft brought a frown and a sneer to his face. It reminded him too vividly of his actual station, and violently dragged him back from the realm of visions he had allowed himself to indulge in. The pirates were busily overhauling their gear, filling water casks, calking dried-out seams, and sluicing opening decks with copiousstreams of water, just as they were used to do in the palmy days when Red Jabez kept them gorged with pillage.

Milo hurried faster, for he feared they too had sighted his ship, and sprang down to the shore to accost surly Caliban.

"Here, Milo old buck, stick yer beak into this, lad!" screamed Caliban, thrusting

28

forward a brimming horn of wine. The giant declined impatiently, waving a hand toward the activity afoot.

"What, won't drink luck, hey?" cried the dwarf, emptying the horn himself. "Ain't got the news yet, hey?"

"News? What news can such as thee have that I am not told?" demanded Milo contemptuously. Caliban scowled viciously at his tone, but the giant's hands were strong, and the little ruffian loved his warped life. He flung down his horn and retorted: "We're to windward o' ye this time, Milo me lad. Th' queen bade us be ready for a lamb headed this way, an', sure enough, there comes a craft now, a'most in sight from here. Small fish, true, but sweet after so long a spell o' famine."

Milo knew that the ship he had seen could not possibly have been detected from the village. It must be yet another craft, and, without a word, he bounded back up the cliff and scanned the waters closer inshore. There, sure enough, lay a beautiful white schooner, her paint dazzling to the eye, her decks flashing with metal, her canvas faultless in fit and set and whiteness. She was still five miles distant and slowly edging along the coast, as if indifferent to her tardy progress. The giant noted her exact position, then presented himself to Dolores.

The girl was luxuriously submitting to the skilful attentions of Pascherette; her wealth of lustrous hair enveloped her like a veil, rendering almost superfluous the filmy silken robe she had donned. But at sight of Milo all her feline contentment fled, and she thrust the maid from her and stood up to receive his report.

"A ship?" she flashed.

"Two, Sultana. The men make ready now."

"The men? Dolt! Did I not tell thee to keep such news for me?"

"They saw the small vessel while I was beyond the Tongue. They have not seen the ship I saw, nor have I told them. It is a great ship, lady; theirs is but a small, poor thing."

"I will see it." Dolores suddenly remembered the maid, whose presence she had ignored. Pascherette stood apart, a small, fairylike French octoroon, dainty as a golden thistledown; her full red lips were parted in eager inquisitiveness, and her slim, small body leaned forward, as if to catch every word; but at sight of her Dolores burst into knowing merriment, for the girl's eyes told her story. They were fastened in intense, burning adoration, not on the mistress but on Milo, the giant slave.

"La-la, chit!" Dolores cried; "keep thy black eyes from my property." But more weighty matters than a maid's fluttering bosom demanded her attention, and she commanded sharply: "Milo, summon the men to the council hall at once. Let none be absent. Go swiftly!" Milo went, and Dolores flashed around on Pascherette again: "And thou, hussy, take this clinging frippery from me and give me my tunic. And, mark me, girl, thy eyes and ears belong to me. Thy tongue, too. Let that tongue utter one word of what those eyes see, those ears hear, and it shall be plucked from thy pretty mouth with hot pincers. Remember!"

Dolores put on her tunic and swept out to steal a long look at the white schooner before entering the hall.

Into the council hall the pirates came trooping, tarry, wet, soiled with the estuary mud as they were, and stood in a milling mob awaiting speech from Dolores, who entered from the rear and scanned their faces closely. Shuffling feet and whistling breath would not be stilled, even in her presence, for their appetites were already whetted for a victim, and the fumes of the previous night's debauch lingered. They glared at the girl and cursed impatiently.

"Hear!" commanded Dolores with an imperious gesture, and every sound was muffled, not stilled. "Hear, my brave jackals! For long ye have hungered for employment fit for the royal corsairs ye are. Now the meal is to hand." The hall reverberated with the clamor that went up. Cutlases scraped from their scabbards and swished aloft; bold Spotted Dog snatched out his great horse-pistol and blazed into the floor, filling the place with acrid smoke and noise. Dolores's eyes flashed angrily; she governed her fury, and went on when the uproar subsided: "Your boats are ready?"

"Ready and rotting wi' idleness!" roared Hanglip.

"And ye purpose wasting powder and shot on some paltry craft of the islands! Wait, my brave lads, I have better game at hand!"

Now the crowd was hushed in earnest, for none of them saw more than a frolic coming from such a small craft as the schooner. The girl went on to tell them of the big ship that Milo had seen, and she painted it a rich West Indiaman, loaded to the hatches with rum and powder, gold and jewels, delicate meats and—with emphasis which she carefully cloaked yet made vivid—dainty ladies, no doubt.

"Take ye the sloop, then," she commanded, "and bring me no tale of failure. Ten miles southwest from the bluff she lies becalmed. Let no man return without tribute for me. Go now!"

With a whoop the evil ruffians tumbled out, hurling themselves pell-mell down to the shore, and splashing out to the boats. Their sloop, a long, beamy Cayman-built craft, of eighty tons and twelve murderous guns that were cast for a king's ship, could be handled by four men or a hundred. She carried fifty men now, and she sped out of the estuary before the faint breeze with a velocity that spelled certain doom for any square-rigged ship she ever lifted over the horizon.

Dolores watched them go with inscrutable face; then commanded Milo to attend her in the great chamber. Pascherette, not yet over her fright, hovered tremblingly near, and her mistress dismissed her with a pacifying pat on the head, flinging, at the same time, a string of pearls around her neck that brought mingled gratitude, greed, and conceit into her sparkling eyes.

"How stands the schooner now?" Dolores asked when the girl had gone.

"She drifts slowly, Sultana. There is little wind. Yet she ever comes nearer."

"Milo, that is my ship!" breathed Dolores fervidly. "I have jewels and silken trash, the richest in my store, which my father told me were taken from such a vessel. A yacht, he called that craft. 'Tis sailed for pleasure; trade never soils the holds of such craft; men who sail such a vessel as that which now hovers near us are of the kind from which comes such as that!" Once more she indicated the "Laughing Cavalier," and now her form and face were filled with surging ambition strengthened with ardent hope.

"How goes our sloop?" she asked abruptly.

"Swiftly, but with the dying breath of the wind. By noon she will be swinging idly, Sultana."

"Who of the boldest rascals remain with us?"

"The noisiest dogs have gone. Sancho remains, for Stumpy cracked his head last night in a brawl. The others here are but cattle!" The giant uttered the words with bitter scorn.

"Then, at noon, Milo, we move to secure my ship!" Dolores cried with gleaming eyes. "Set slaves to move out the false Point and anchor it a cable-length off the true. I will have a plan then to lure the schooner on. We must not let her escape, Milo!"

"Pardon, lady, I know a way!"

"And that?"

"I will swim to the schooner and command them to thy presence."

Dolores smiled whimsically, for she was too wise to be ignorant of the fact that such men as were in that schooner must first be caught before they might be commanded. Yet the giant's plan suggested another to her.

"Hear my plan," she said. "That chit—Pascherette—she's a dainty minx! Does she swim?"

"Like a conger, Sultana!" Milo's face lighted warmly, and Dolores shrewdly guessed then that the *petite* octoroon's regard for the giant was not altogether unrequited.

31

"Then carry her abreast of the vessel,quickly, and bid her swim out to it. Let her use some of the cunning that is in her pretty little head, and make them wonder what else our island has to offer in dainties. Then, ere evening, I shall have work for thee that shall complete what Pascherette begins. Command the minx to bring forth all her fascinations and allurements. Nay, friend, have no fear for thy sweetheart. I warrant thee she can care for herself, if she will. Go! It is my command!"

Milo departed, and Dolores went out to the Grove, climbed nimbly to the clifftop, and sat down to watch. She had a clear view of the schooner now winging lazily along three miles away and a mile off shore; the shore, from the point where her rascals were even now towing out a great mass of interlaced trees and foliage planted upon stout logs to form a false point, right along to abreast of the schooner, lay immediately beneath her eye; the blue sea glittered and flashed under the hot sun, unruffled by wind, and only bursting into a long line of creamy foam, where it licked the golden sands. The tall palms nodded languorously, their deep green heads faintly chafing like sleeping crickets; the tinkle of the sands came up to her ears like tiny bells.

Dolores followed with her eyes two swiftly moving figures on the shore path, hidden from the ocean by a mass of verdure, and she smiled cryptically. The giant Milo strode on his way like the embodiment of force; at his side tripped Pascherette, her glossy black crown barely reaching above his waist, her tiny hand hidden completely in his great fist. And she kept her bright eyes raised to his great height all the while, satisfied that her little feet should trip, perhaps, if only her eyes tripped not from his face.

Presently they stopped, and Dolores stood up alertly. There was but a moment's delay, while Pascherette bound her hair more securely; then, with a flirting hand-wave, the little octoroon darted from Milo, wriggled through the bushes, and ran lightly down to the sea. In another moment her small, black head was moving rapidly toward the schooner, her golden skin flashing warmly in the sun as her arms swept over and over in an adept stroke that carried her forward with the speed of a fish.

CHAPTER VI.

THE PARTY FROM THE YACHT.

The schooner yacht Feu Follette swam sluggishly along shore, her lofty canvas flapping in the faint air. On her spotless quarter-deck, Rupert Venner, wealthy idler and owner of the vessel, lounged in a deck-chair a picture of the utter finality of boredom. His guests, Craik Tomlin and John Pearse, made perfunctory pretense of admiring the lovely coast scenery along the port hand; but their air was that of men surfeited with sights, tired of the languorous calm, *blasé* of life.

The schooner's appointments typified money in abundance. From forecastle capstan to binnacle she glowed and glittered with massive brass and ornate gilding; along the waist six burnished-bronze cannon stood on heavily carved carriages, lashings and breechings as white as a shark's tooth; over the quarter-deck double awnings gave ample clearance to the swing of the main boom—the outer of dazzling white canvas, the inner of richest, striped silk-and-cotton mixture. The open doors of the deckhouse companion revealed an interior of ivory paneling touched with gold, and hung with heavy velvet punkahs. The walls were embellished with exactly the right number of art gems to establish the artistic perception of the owner and to whet the expectation for more yet unseen. But, with all this, the Feu Follette housed a discontented master and discontented guests.

"Oh, for a breeze!" grumbled Pearse, breaking in on the frowning silence. "How much longer are we to drift around these stagnant seas, Venner?"

"The very next slant of wind shall wing us homeward," replied Venner dreamily. "I, too, am sick of the cruise and its deadly monotony."

Again silence, marred only by creak of gear and flap of idle sails. The schooner barely moved now, though the western sky held promise of a breeze later on. Then came a cry from one of the negro crewforward, and its tenor stirred the party into mild interest.

"De debbil, ef 'tain't one o' dem marmaids! Oh, Cæsar!"

A ripple of panting laughter alongside brought Venner and his guests to the rail in haste, and gone to the windless heavens was their ennui. A gleaming, gold-tinted creature, a miniature model of Aphrodite surely, arose from the blue sea and climbed nimbly into the main channels and thence to the deck, where little pools of water dripped from the radiant figure. She shook her small head saucily, and heavy masses of raven-wing hair tumbled about her, provokingly cloaking the charms so boldly outlined by her single saturated tunic of fine silk.

"Who in paradise may you be?" ejaculated Venner, while his friends stared with unconscious rudeness.

"I? I am Pascherette!" laughed the small vision, and her black eyes sparkled impudently.

"Pascherette!" echoed Tomlin, bewildered. "Does Jamaica hold such beauties?" He awkwardly brought forward a deck-chair, while Pearse stood by in speechless amazement. Venner, as better became the host, ordered a steward to bring a wrap for the astounding visitor, but the girl laughed provokingly and declined both.

"It is not for such as I, fine gentlemen," she said, and her sharp eyes were roving busily about the schooner, appraising values like a veritable pirate. "Keep thy courtesies for better than I."

"Better than you, girl?" Venner's tone was incredulous. He was taking mental stock of the priceless pearls about Pascherette's dainty throat. "To be found here?"

"If not here, where shall ye find such a one as my mistress?" Pascherette retorted saucily.

"Your mistress?"

"Without doubt. I am but a slave, my lady is the queen, Dolores."

"A queen—a white woman?" stammered Venner.

"Oh, Venner, let us look into this!" exclaimed Pearse with unconcealed curiosity.

"Just what we have prayed for!" Tomlin supplemented eagerly. "Anchor, Venner, like a good fellow. A jaunt ashore will brace us all up."

"Nonsense!" objected the owner, albeit with a good trace of inquisitiveness himself. "The breeze will come by evening; and who knows what this coast harbors? A bad name sticks to this shore."

Pascherette had wandered forward, and between sly glances aft and keen scrutiny shoreward, she flung seductive smiles broadcast at the grinning crew, prattling prettily to officer and man alike, as if she were indeed a stranger to the ways of shipboard. While she made her rounds the party aft entered into a warm dispute; their curiosity was whetted, but not sufficiently in Venner's case, to whom the safety of the yacht was paramount just then. They wrangled for half an hour, and the schooner drifted on until she was within a mile or so of the outflung false Point. Then they were again startled out of their self-possession—this time by a cry from the girl who leaned over the bulwarks a picture of ardent admiration for something in the water.

Double awnings and snowy hammock-cloths restricted the view shoreward from the quarter-deck chairs, and surprise as deep as that which greeted the girl surged through the disputing three at a great splashing over the side, accompanied by the boom of a voice that must come from a powerful, free-breathing chest.

"Room for Milo, servant of Dolores!" the hail rang out, and by the same means as Pascherette had used, up climbed Milo, to stand motionless before the white men, an astounding and awe-inspiring shape.

"Another slave of the mysterious queen?" demanded Venner, when recovered from his astonishment. "It gets interesting, gentlemen. And what is your errand, Goliath?" he inquired of Milo.

"I know no Goliath. I am Milo. I come to summon ye to the presence of my queen," returned the giant with as much unconcern as if he were inviting the pirates to a barbecue.

A titter of amusement passed over the three yachtsmen. It was tinged with resentment, though, and only curiosity, aroused by shock upon shock, preventedan angry rejoinder to Milo's speech that could only have ended one way: in physical damage to three idle gentlemen of wealth and pleasure.

"A summons, hey?" scoffed Tomlin. "Your queen values her rank, I think." A dangerous gleam crept into Milo's eyes, and Pearse detected it in time. "Venner," he said quietly, "you cannot let this adventure pass. Here's every element of sport held up to us. Let us obey this command, and get at least a thrill out of this humdrum cruise."

Venner was thinking of many things, and his mind needed little making up. He had never lost sight of those pearls of Pascherette's; his eye could not be deceived; they were priceless. And Pearse had not failed to notice the green jade skull-charm that depended from Milo's columnar neck, a jade skull with pearls for teeth like the altar brooch of Dolores. And Tomlin, for all his expressed scorn, was tingling with ardent desire for such piquant beauty and vivacity as Pascherette's. If such a creature were the slave, then what could the mistress be? He assumed a more complaisant attitude, and added his vote: "A good way of passing away this odious calm spell, Venner. Let us go."

"Where is this great queen, my Colossus?" Venner asked.

"I will lead thee to her presence," replied Milo. "Thy boat will take us there in a few moments. Further on, beyond that point, the ship may lie safely in the haven."

Venner called his sailing master, and together they examined the chart. It showed a sand-bar stretching off the point, a deep-water channel, narrow but accessible, close to.

"You can work into that anchorage?" asked Venner.

"Yes, sir, if the air don't die away altogether. It seems good ground by the chart."

"Then carry the schooner in and bring up. Call away my cutter, and"—in an undertone—"keep a good watch, Peters, this is an evil coast."

The shrill pipes reverberated under the awnings, and sailors, neat and trim in white uniforms that contrasted beautifully with their dark skins, ran to man the graceful white cutter. Pascherette sat in the stern-sheets, cuddled up like a pretty kitten on a crimson silk cushion, and Milo stood erect, as firm as if on solid ground, between passengers and rowers as the boat sped shoreward. As the two craft separated the schooner stood out in veritable beauty, an exquisite thing of gold and ivory, pearl and rose. Venner's eyes lighted with pride at sight of her. Even a long, eventless cruise had not killed the artist in him. He touched Milo softly on the thigh and said with a smile:

"Has your queen anything like that, my friend?"

Milo cast a disdainful glance at the yacht, abruptly turned away again, and replied shortly: "That is nothing."

"Nothing!" said Venner. "Then where have you seen daintier work of men's hands and brains?"

"Thou shall see. Thy ship is a petty thing."

"Now, by Heaven, Venner, he has you there!" laughed Tomlin, never ceasing for a moment from ogling Pascherette, who purred with contentment and smiled slyly at the frown that came to Milo's face.

"Oh, yes, a poor thing!" laughed Pascherette, hugging her knees and rippling over with amusement. "My mistress is a great queen. These"—touching her pearls—"thy rigging could be formed of such, if my queen willed."

"And in the house of such a great queen, my girl, are doubtless other things of beauty and worth?" put in Venner with growing sarcasm.

"As witness this pretty wench!" smiled Tomlin, striving to fix the girl's capricious attention, which persisted in flying ever to Milo.

"Patience," returned Milo. "Do ye know of anything of untold worth—my queen has that which will buy it? Have ye seen a thing of peerless beauty—in my queen's house are many of its peers! Patience!"

No word more would the giant utter. Like a bronze statue he stood erect, guiding the cutter to a small landing with a silent gesture. And as the boat swept alongside and the yachtsmen began to experience the thrill of near expectancy, Pearse caught sight of a knot of men loitering on the nearby slopes, and their appearance startled him.

"Good Lord, look at those piratical ruffians!" he cried.

His companions started, and doubt came into their faces. Then Pascherette arose from her seat and pressed near to Tomlin, with an insinuating, caressing movement; and that ardent gentleman exclaimed impatiently: "Oh, never mind their looks! Come on Venner! This is what I've dreamed of all my life! Come on!"

Milo touched Pearse's arm, said briefly, "Come!" and that reluctant visitor stepped ashore; while Venner, after a little twinge of misgiving, succumbed to his curiosity regarding the hidden glories of this strange realm, and followed the great black readily enough.

Up the cliff they followed Milo, Pascherette running ahead and looking backward ever and again with a seductive gesture of invitation; and in good time they stood before the council hall, the loitering pirates staring at them wonderingly, and from them to the graceful white schooner just then entering the narrow channel.

"Enter!" said Milo, and stood aside at the open door.

The interior was dark and awfully still, and the three white men paused on the threshold doubtfully, regarding each other with half-ashamed faces.

"Enter!" reiterated Milo, and curiosity got the better of them, for a swirl of fragrance eddied out to them, and one by one, until the hall was dotted with them, ruby and amber lights twinkled before them, seeming to beckon them on to something mysterious in the shadows beyond the soft lights.

"Neck or nothing!" muttered Venner, leading the way. His friends followed in silence. Then the doors closed behind them; but fear, doubt, unbelief, all went to the winds at the spectacle that slowly unfolded itself before their gaze.

"Cleopatra reincarnated, by God!" gasped Venner. His friends could find no words to express their sensations in that moment.

Dolores glided out from the heavy hangings behind her chair of state, and stood, a vision of majestic loveliness, on the dais. Clad in her short tunic, her hair bound to her brow by the gold circlet that Milo had made, she had calculated effects with the art of a Circe. Her rounded arms and bare shoulders, faultless throat and swelling bosom, radiant enough in their own fair perfection, she had embellished with such jewels as subtly served to accentuate even that perfection. Upon one polished forearm a bracelet was pressed, a gaud formed from one immense emerald cut in a fash-

37

ion that forced one to doubt the existence of such a cutter in mortal form. About her neck a rope of exquisitely matched black pearls supported a single uncut emerald which might have been born in the same matrix with that on her arm. Her red leather sandals were fastened, and her ankles crisscrossed, with such bands of glittering fire as a goddess might have stolen from the belt of Orion.

These things were revealed gradually by cunningly manipulated light effects until Dolores blazed out entire before her stupefied guests. They, seeking for relief from the spell, sought in her face some answer to the riddle; but her expression was that of a being apart: tantalizingly, inscrutably indifferent to their presence. Then Milo advanced, prostrated himself before her, and reported his errand done. "Rise, Milo, and I thank thee," she said, and her soft, yet vibrant, voice sent a thrill through her waiting guests. Dolores waved a hand toward the door. "Send Sancho in to me at once, Milo, and do ye watch for the return of my wolves."

The giant went out; yet the calm face of Dolores gave no relief to the three yachtsmen; uneasiness began to sit heavily upon them, and it was not lessened by the entry of Sancho, for such an awful impersonation of evil in one man they had never seen before.

"Sancho," Dolores commanded him, "it is my will that the vessel now entering my haven be cared for as mine. See to it!"

"The lads are hungry, lady; it is long since they tasted such—" Sancho snarled his protest with wickedly curling lips that revealed ragged yellow fangs. Dolores stared him down with blazing eyes, held his gaze for a breath and uttered: "Go! See to it! Thy life is the bond!" and Sancho slunk out like a whipped cur.

There was an uncanny hint of dynamic force in the girl's swift assumption of authority, and Tomlin found his throat very dry despite the fact that he was drinking greedily of her beauty. Venner stole a look at Pearse, and saw in that gentleman a reflection of his own rising uneasiness. And then, at that instant of shivery doubt, Dolores smiled at them; and in that same instant three men, with immortal souls, forgot everything of the world and affairs in the mad intoxication of her charm.

"Welcome, sirs," she smiled, and stepped down to offer each a hand in turn—not in handshake, but with an air that said plainly homage was due to her; and whether he would or not, each of her guests raised the hand to his lips with reverence.

"What is your pleasure, lady?" asked Venner quietly. He was resolved to show his friends the way into this magnificent creature's intimate confidence; and the resolution promised interesting developments, for each of his friends nursed a similar one. There was, even now, less of comradeship in the looks with which the friends

38

regarded each other. If Dolores detected this, she made no sign. She gave a hand to Venner, led him to the door, and smiled invitation to the others. They followed hungrily.

"I will give thee food and wine," she said; "then I have much to say to thee. I have commanded that thy ship and thy men be cared for; to-night ye are my guests. Come! But first give me thy swords. Thou'rt with friends." They complied dumbly, dazed by her radiant charm.

They stepped outside into the glaring sunlight; a light breeze was now singing in the tall palms and making silvery music of the wavelets along the shore; far away to the southwest a sliver of sail was in sight, and to a practised eye could be made out as the pirate sloop returning. Dolores glanced swiftly around, seeking some evidence that her commands to Sancho were being obeyed; but she saw no man—no figure save the ancient crone she had discarded and sent to the drudgery of the kitchen. With a keen sidelong glance she saw that the schooner was heavily grounded on the Point; a second glance told her that her guests were thinking little of the schooner, for their eyes never left her face. But notice was forced upon them, and the reason for the camp's desertion impressed upon her, by the weird, drawn-out scream of jubilation that issued from the old woman's withered throat an instant before her old eyes gave her sight of her mistress and froze the cry at her lips.

"Ha, ha, ha!" she shrieked, waving skinny arms. "That's the way Red Jabez taught his lambs! Flesh your blade, my bully Rufe, and bring me some of the meat!"

Abruptly Dolores's guests swung around to follow the direction of the old woman's arm, and the girl darted a look of fury at the scene. Out from the point poured Yellow Rufe and a horde of strange mulattos and blacks, and shots crackled from the schooner's rails. On the little bay two boats filled with Sancho and his men pulled frantically toward the fight, and the haven rang with howls of gleeful anticipation. Venner uttered a smoking oath, and clutched Tomlin and Pearse by the arms.

"Come fellows!" he cried. "This is treachery!"

"Treachery? Ye wrong me, sirs!" Dolores's soft voice halted them. They stared at her, and she gave them back look for look until she saw the blood surge back to their faces and their eyes lose their hardness. Then she laughed, low and sweet, and waved them back.

"Wait. I shall preserve thy ship, and give thee back an eye for an eye if thy men are harmed. Trust me, will ye not?" She paused a moment to thrill them with her eyes; they stayed. Then she sped down the cliff like a deer.

CHAPTER VII.

THE ATTACK ON THE FEU FOLLETTE.

By means of the floating blind the Point had been carried out across the narrow channel until its edge rested on the bar; and the schooner lay with a heavy list broadside on to the hard sand. Yellow Rufe and his followers, runaways from the pirates' camp, maroons banished from their homes for crimes against their fellows, rebellious slaves, and what not, splashed through the shallow water and stormed the Feu Follette by way of the jib-boom and head-rigging, while Sancho urged his boats on toward the vessel's quarters.

Dolores, uncertain yet as to Sancho's motives, but in no uncertainty as to Rufe's, paused but to look around for Milo as she leaped down the cliff. The giant was even then engaged in thwarting an inclination on the part of the yachtsmen to follow Dolores, for, her spell gone for the moment, Venner felt all an owner's solicitude for his property. But Milo had been well schooled;he knew how to play upon little weaknesses; Pascherette had told him, if he had not seen for himself, how amorousness and cupidity formed the key-note of character in the visitors; and now he used the knowledge to the fullest extent. The little octoroon appeared as Dolores watched; she had hastily attired herself in dry clothes, a single garment more filmy and daring than that she had worn to swim aboard the schooner, and from her mistress's store had borrowed jewels that transformed her into a beautiful little golden butterfly.

Dolores saw all this in a flash; she saw Pascherette take capable charge of the three men, led them away from the cliff, and then Milo advanced to the steep path. Turning swiftly to resume her career, Dolores uttered a shrill, piercing cry that the giant understood perfectly, and she plunged into the sea as he bounded down the slope to her support.

The schooner's crew were already hard pressed; but they fought like men, led courageously by Peters, the sailing master. As Dolores cleft the sparkling water, speeding out to them like a gorgeous sprite of the waves, men tugged at gun-tack-

40

les to swing a piece around to rake their own decks, for Yellow Rufe and his ruffians had swept the forecastle clear of defenders. And Dolores reached the vessel, climbed over the low-listing rail nimbly as a jungle cat, at the instant when Sancho's boats hooked on to the main-chains and took the crew in the rear.

The pirate queen stood for a single long breath to grasp the scene in its entirety. Panting slightly from her exertions, her blazing eyes and heaving breast rendered her a figure of bewildering and awful loveliness; and the Feu Follette's men paused in the fight out of sheer amazement.

Sancho's gaze fell on her the moment his evil head topped the rail, and into his eyes crept an expression of detected insubordination. He sought Yellow Rufe, but Dolores had seen all she needed to apprise her that this was a concerted attempt to flout her authority. Then Rufe's hoarse roar went up, and the tide of struggling men surged anew, and Sancho, plucking up heart, rejoined with a scream.

"Into the sea with the dogs!" he cried. "'Tis such a craft as Jabez would love to see ye carry."

The fight rolled aft, and Dolores was left standing alone by the midship shot-rack. She singled out a few of her men by name, and commanded them to rally to her side; then, seizing a cutlas from the deck, she glided tigerishly to the main companionway, down which the pirates were now driving the beaten crew, and the men she had picked out were shorn of all indecision as Milo leaped on board with a bull-throated shout and gained her side.

"Sancho! Rufe! Have done with this play!" she cried, placing herself in front of the blood-hungry horde. "Dogs, fall back! Have ye no memory that ye forget how Dolores strikes?"

Milo had picked up a handspike, and with it across his breast he bore back the scowling rascals, smiling the while himself with quiet contempt. But one, hardier than the rest, ran to the skylight, dashed in the glass with his boot, and cried with outflung arm:

"A plague upon her and her strokes. See yonder, lads—her cunning trick—our sloop comes back empty-handed, as she well knew it would—and here lies to your hands work that the Red Chief had reveled in. Down with her and the big bull! Below is loot fit for bold fellows."

Without moving from where he stood, Milo pivoted around, the heavy handspike—six feet of true ash—rigid as a bar of iron, took the overbold pirate at the base of the skull and spilled his brains into the breach he had made. Growling with fury, a man from Sancho's crew sprang to avenge the stroke with steel, and his blade creased down Milo's sturdy ribs before the giant had recovered from his own

41

swing. And with the hissing slit of ripping skin Milo's debt was paid for him. Dolores, agile as a panther, reached the pirate with her cutlas pointed, and the steel hilt rang against his breast-bone.

But in the momentary pause in her vigilance, a score of Rufe's ruffians burst past her and poured below into the saloon, where renewed sounds of combat told of the ferreting out of the beaten crew.

"Milo, follow me!" cried Dolores, springing down the stairs herself, careless whether her wavering half-dozen followed or stayed. Her whole soul was sickened with the fear that this vessel, the long-wished-for means of her release from what had become a hateful bondage, was in danger of destruction at the red hands of Rufe's undisciplined dogs. And swiftly approaching on the freshening evening breeze her sloop grew momentarily clearer to the eye; it was easy to fancy she could hear the howls of disappointed rage pealing up from her deck; it needed no second sight to determine the side those humiliated pirates would take, when they hove alongside another prey which promised at least a taste of coveted loot.

In the brief time since the pirates' entry the schooner's saloon had become a place of desolation. All the magnificence of unrestricted cost was there; and all the beauty of artistic selection; and over all was the mark of the beast—blood and torn hangings, corpses and splintered panels, chaos and sulfur smoke as the pillage started. Dolores sought out through the smoke a breathing man in the uniform of the yacht, and swiftly placed her lips to his ear, her mind made up to a terrible expedient to save this vessel for herself.

"Tell me quickly—where is the magazine?"

The man opened his agonized eyes, saw that splendid blazing face close to his own, and shook his head loyally. He would give his master's enemies no assistance.

"Speak, fool!" she hissed, shaking him. They were alone by the great table-leg on the red-stained carpet. "I would defeat these sharks! Where is the powder?"

The man looked into her eyes again, and she smiled at him. It was enough. He weakly pointed to a stout door on the starboard side, forward of the sailing master's stateroom door, beyond which the sound of axes already resounded. The owner's and guests' quarters were filled to overflowing with ravenous wolves tearing and ripping in a frenzy of pillage. At the after-end of the saloon a pirate stood over a great cask, issuing jugs of liquor to such of his fellows as found time amid the riot to drink. Milo gripped his handspike, waiting for a command that should send him like awful Fate into the thick of the murderous mob.

"Milo! Bring me a powder-keg from that magazine!" Dolores said, still crouching low and hidden beneath the smoke-pall. The giant entered the room, shattering

42

the lock with a lunge of his shoulder, and returned bearing an unopened keg of cannon powder.

"Place it upon the table." Then the girl rose to her feet with eyes glittering coldly and lips pressed to a tight line. "Find me a lighted brand—swiftly!" she said, and when the giant snatched up a splinter of dry wood, lighting it at the steward's brazier in the little pantry off the saloon, she swept majestically aft to suddenly confront the roaring ruffian at the wine cask.

"Milo, hurl this liquor cask away!"

Milo picked up the heavy barrel as a man might pick up a cushion, heaved it above his head, and flung it like a cannon-shot at the door, behind which rang the greatest noise, while the pirate, whose care the wine had been, gaped like a stranded fish.

"Now this dog!"

The man followed his cask before his mouth closed from his astonishment; but as he flew his leathern lungs performed their office and warned the pillagers of peril. Out from cabins and storerooms poured the rascals, gorged with fine wines and delicate foods seized in their pillaging; steamy with blood not yet dried on their bestial faces. And when the great saloon was full, Dolores raised her torch above her head and blazed out at them:

"In five short breaths this vessel carries all thy black souls to hell! Skulking rats, swim while the breath is in you!"

The torch came down, Milo smashed in the head of the keg, revealing the terrible contents, and as if in grim jest he snatched up a sprinkling of the powder and flicked some grains into the flare of the torch. If there had been any doubt as to the deadly earnestness of Dolores, there could be none now, for sparks crackled and spit in fearful nearness to that open keg. Men stampeded for the stairs, hurling each other down in their frenzy; but Yellow Rufe and Sancholingered. Theirs had been the gravest fault; if they fled, it must be only to do penance some other day; if they forced Dolores's hand, at least she and that scornful giant must die the death also. They stood their ground, staring defiantly into her expressionless face.

Dolores spoke no word more. Milo stood like a bronze figure of Doom at her side, his noble face expressionless as hers. Between them stood that keg of terrible possibilities. The girl lowered the torch until the flame all but licked the wood of the keg; a dropping piece of charred wood fell audibly against the side. Sancho's breath caught painfully; Yellow Rufe's bloodshot eyes wavered. Still they held on.

"Milo, I give thee freedom!" said Dolores in a low, distinct voice that carried to their ears like the sound of a silver bell. "Farewell, faithful friend!"

43

The torch swept around, fanning to a blaze in the eddying air, then darted toward the keg. And with a yell that echoed on deck and far out over the sea, Yellow Rufe and Sancho turned and fled, fighting with each other, as had their less bold fellows, for the precious air of safety.

Dolores laughed contemptuously, flung the torch aside and bade Milo trample it out, then she, too, ascended to the deck to view her victory. The sea was dotted with swimming men, the beach was full of running men, terrified men made the cliff resound with their cries. Then, sure that the schooner was free of foes, Dolores looked toward the sloop, now within hail of the schooner and coming fast with sail and sweeps, while her crew stared over the low bulwarks in puzzlement as to the reason for the hasty exodus from the strange craft.

"Here, Milo, is fresh fare of trouble. Hast brought my own flag?"

"Here, Sultana," replied Milo, taking a carefully folded silken banner from a pocket in his leathern tunic.

"Hoist it, then, at the main! Perhaps Hanglip and Caliban, Stumpy and the rest of my brave jackals, will forego their expected meal at sight of it. And send forth a shout for slaves; this vessel must be cleansed and her people's wounds attended to."

Up at the schooner's lofty main-truck the Sultana's private flag fluttered out; the mark and sign of Dolores's ownership. And while three anxious yachtsmen on the cliff-top waited for her return, a hundred and twenty hungry and thirsty baffled ruffians on the sloop cursed her vehemently in their hoarse, dry throats.

CHAPTER VIII.

DOLORES DELIVERS JUDGMENT.

On the level sward before the village the three yachtsmen paced back and forth in an ecstasy of apprehension. Pascherette had left them, after playing them like fish with her own charms and a hinted promise of Dolores's favors as bait; and the moment they were alone Venner shook off the spell in a resurging determination to attend to the safety of his vessel in person.

"Follow me, Pearse; come Tomlin!" he said. "We are three mad fools to stand here while these pirates loot and wreck the Feu Follette!"

Tomlin shuddered as he started to follow. Pearse kept silence, but did not hesitate. But they had not stepped ten paces before they realized fully the completeness of their helplessness, for Venner, first to attempt the path down, was brought to a halt by a musket leveled at his breast, the musketeer showing only his head and shoulders above the cliff edge. And as Tomlin and Pearse came up, they, too, were abruptly halted in like manner; and a grinning Carib motioned each back with an unspoken command which was none the less inexorable.

They returned to their first positions, and resumed their nervous walk, condemning themselves as utter idiots for venturing unarmed into such a nest of vipers at the urge of curiosity, novelty, feminine attraction, greed—whatever their motives had been. And here Dolores came upon them, while all about them swarmed the disgruntled pirates from the sloop, and those of the mutineers whose abject fears warned them to take whatever punishment their queen chose to mete out rather than toescape only to be brought back to endure penalties immeasurably more terrible.

Yellow Rufe and Sancho were not minded to stay, however; they had vanished; and Dolores's keen eyes noted this the moment she surveyed the scene. She walked swiftly to the door of the council hall, turned to face the mob, and lifted an arm for attention. Then fell a hush full of anxiety or terror, according to the degree of culpability in the consciousness of her audience.

"Summon every creature in the village," she cried, "and let no man or woman dare to leave this place until ye hear my thoughts concerning this day's work!"

Men scattered eagerly through the huts, calling by name all who were not present in the crowd, and presently more of the community came out, their faces mostly reflecting the terror that was in their souls; for none might ever foretell the moods of their queen. Inscrutable as night, her eyes were like pools of violet shadow wherein lurked promise or threat of unimaginable things; every line of her face and form was a line of a riddle that could prove in the solution either magnificent generosity, fearless justice, or implacable vengeance: like the lightning, Dolores struck where she willed, and in what fashion she chose; it was useless to attempt avoidance.

Venner and his friends looked on curiously, a feeling akin to awe pervading them at the increasing evidence before their eyes of the power wielded by this splendid fury, they had yet to know. When all were present, except those whose activities on the schooner had already procured them a passport to another world, Dolores swept the crowd with a penetrating glance and called for Milo, who appeared from the rear of the council hall laden with chains and bilboes which he cast down at her feet. Then the angry impatience of the disappointed sloop's crew proved too intense, and Caliban bounded to the front, squealing shrilly:

"The fiend may take you with your irons! Shall we, men who followed Red Jabez through a sea of blood, cower to a woman of such soft mettle? Dolores, queen or woman or wench, it is for you, not us, to explain. Lads—" he shrieked, flashing about and haranguing his companions—"back me in this. We will know why the sloop lacked powder; why to-day's work has brought no reward!"

The deformed little demon stepped back to the crowd, and paced to and fro with feverish gestures, scowling blackly at every turn that brought him face to face with Dolores. The packed mob milled and murmured, some afraid, many of Caliban's mind yet not daring to openly support him. Venner and his friends sensed the thrill of it, for their brief experience of the pirate queen left them in slight doubt as to the outcome of Caliban's speech. Dolores herself stood motionless for a full minute after the hunchback ceased his defiance, and under her lowered, heavily lashed eyelids the dark eyes seemed to slumber; only in her lips was any trace of the alertness that governed her brain, and those scarlet petals, which seemed to have been plucked from a love flower in the garden of passion, slowly, almost imperceptibly parted, until the dazzling teeth gleamed through in a smile that none might yet determine whether soft or terrible. And as the seconds heaped suspense upon suspense, the overbold Caliban was seized with a choking fear that he was to pay the price. Then Dolores spoke, slowly, quietly, almost soothingly; and those of her hardened ruffians who thought they knew her best hung on her words in shivery uncertainty.

"For those bold words, Caliban, my father had stripped thy poisonous skin from thy putrid flesh. Yesterday thy queen might not have proved more merciful. Yet do I know how thy disappointment chafes thy brave soul, and because of that thy rash speech goes unpunished." The hush intensified, for the leniency of Dolores was little less to be feared than her fury. A smile of ineffable radiance broke over her beautiful face, and she extended her right hand and said, still in the same slow, even voice: "Come, Caliban. Thou art worthy of my mercy. Kneel, that I may know thy heart is right."

Now the suspense reached its climax. Somewhere behind those softly spoken words surely lurked some awful, cunninglycloaked threat. Caliban went white, ghastly; his brave tongue stuck to his palate, and the thin lips slavered with growing panic.

"Come, Caliban!"

The girl's command was uttered no louder, her expression was unchanged; in her glorious eyes gleamed no trace of anything other than benign forgiveness; she remained motionless as before, with her rounded arm and shapely hand extended in a manner that revealed their every perfection.

"Come, Caliban!"

Again the words fell from her smiling lips, and now the quivering hunchback obeyed, drawn irresistibly by her magnetism, sick with dread of the stroke he in common with all his mates expected to fall.

"Kneel! See, I give thee my hand to kiss," Dolores said, and smiled upon the cowering wretch with a tender brilliance that sent a tremendous flutter through the hearts of the three yachtsmen.

Caliban knelt and took the proffered hand, then at her word he stood before her, scarcely certain yet that his head was solidly established on his shoulders. She motioned him to stand on one side of her, then, aglow with warm color, she addressed the puzzled throng:

"My bold sea tigers, the ship that escaped thy sloop is but one ship. The seas are full of such. Yet, until to-day, how many have ye been forced to let go because of thy poor equipment in craft? Thy sloop, how small, how old—yet what rich prey escaped thy guns since the Red Chief's swift brig laid her bones here? None! Yet ye complain because I prevented thee destroying the beautiful schooner the gods have this day sent to us!"

Now the purport of her speech struck home; the seemingly soft-brained weakness that had forbidden the rape and pillage of the schooner stood in part explained. And as the light filtered through thick skulls and shone upon all but atrophied brains, a deep muttering swelled into the embryo of a throaty cheer that needed but one look of encouragement from Dolores to spring into noisy life. As for Venner, his expression was reflected in Tomlin, and both in Pearse; and awakening or resurrected, fear was the keynote of all.

"The vampire means to suck us dry after all!" whispered Venner hoarsely. His friends could only squeeze his arm in mute sympathy. They harbored no doubts at all.

Dolores went on:

"With such a vessel as this"—pointing to the schooner—"that Indiaman to-day had never shown heels. And more, how think ye my store is replenished? Dost think I tap the rock for wine? Does Milo crush the granite and bring forth meat for thy hungry bellies? Are my treasures kept at high tide by snatching the colors from the sunset? Fools!" she cried, and for a moment passion conquered her calm. "In that schooner are wines that will make thy hot blood living flame; meats that will put teeth into the throats of the toothless; treasures fit for thy queen's treasury. And more to thy hand, my brave jackals, those pretty pieces of ordnance, which the sun even now paints with liquid gold, will outrange the guns of a king's ship." Pausing, she bent upon the murmuring crew a look of blazing majesty; then concluded with a vibrant demand: "Now dost know why thy queen withheld thy senseless hands from witless destruction?"

Her question was scarcely heard before the answer came. From a hundred rusty throats pealed a huzzah that rolled out over the sea and sent the sea-birds squawking with fright to more peaceful surroundings.

"Dolores! Dolores! That's a queen for the tribe of Jolly Roger!" howled Hanglip, and tumult rang again.

The girl raised her hand, and silence fell once more.

"Hear my judgment upon such of ye as are not of thy mind," she cried, and now the smile had gone; her eyes flashed and the words fell red-hot from her scornful lips.

"I demand no tales from thy mouths. Hiding among these woods Yellow Rufe and Sancho, he of the one eye and the mutilated hand, think to ward off my vengeance. By meridian to-morrow I command those traitors to be brought to me. Fail in this, and ye shall see that Dolores can be terrible, too."

The crowd took this as a dismissal, and broke into parties to scour the woods. Only slaves and women remained, and Pascherette ran to her mistress's side and whispered, with a sidelong look of coquettish allurement at Venner and his friends.

"Something about to happen!" Venner whispered, hoping that it might prove something in recompense for his day of stress. Dolores cast a look of cool indifference toward them and told Milo:

"Put these strangers in separate chambers, Milo. Iron them securely and look to it well. Thou art answerable for them."

No more. She took Pascherette and departed.

CHAPTER IX.

THE SULTANA DECIDES SEVERAL THINGS.

There was a moment of cruel amazement for Venner and the others when Dolores had gone; then Milo, approaching with his irons and chains, awoke the captives to resistance.

"No chains for me, by God!" shouted Venner, crouching to ward off the giant's approach. "Tomlin, Pearse, break for the schooner! I'll hold this savage. We shall perhaps fail; but by the powers of justice we'll go down fighting on our own ship!"

He sprang at Milo as he spoke, and his friends hesitated. Milo, without haste, without change of countenance, dropped his irons and reached Venner with great deliberate strides. And in that momentary hesitation Tomlin and Pearse were lost with their host; for the giant stretched out one tremendous arm, seized Venner by the slack breast of his shirt, and lifted him from the ground, flailing with both hands like some puny child in the grip of his nurse.

Milo spoke no word. He gave no more attention to Venner's futile blows than to the whispering of the sands of the shore. But bearing ever toward the other two men, now seemingly paralyzed out of all volition by the awful exhibition of strength, he reached out with his free hand and added Tomlin to his capture as he had taken Venner.

Pearse might even now have made his bid for liberty; but he was no coward to desert his companions. He uttered a choking cry of mingled fear and defiance, and rushed in between his friends to swing a heavy blow with his fist fair upon the giant's unprotected temple. Now Milo gave sign of interest. He laughed: a deep, rumbling, pleasant laugh of appreciation for the courage that prompted the blow; but he never blinked at the impact, nor did he attempt to avoid another blow that came swiftly. Simply putting forth a greater effort of muscle he swung his two captives apart, held them at arm's length while the sinews of his mighty chest and beam-like arms writhed and rippled like snakes, and rushed upon Pearse with the terrible resistlessness of an avalanche. A shower of blows pounded his face and breast as

50

he closed, then he laughed again; this time triumphantly; for Pearse was enfolded between Venner and Tomlin in a hug that spelled suffocation did he persist in his struggles.

The swift conquest had taken but minutes; none but a few women of the camp had seen it; and they, well used to such scenes, simply chattered and smiled pityingly, not with pity for the men, but for the futility of their resistance. Milo, scarcely breathing above normal, called loudly: "Pascherette!" and gave his prisoners another quieting squeeze.

Pascherette was with her mistress. She did not answer, and Milo called again: "Pascherette!"

The other women drew near, and on many a wickedly fair face shone a light of hope that its wearer might serve in Pascherette's place, no matter what the errand; for it was not the *petite* golden octoroon alone who had sighed for love of the giant.

"Pascherette is with the Sultana, Milo. Let me answer for her," spoke out a dark beauty whose sparkling eyes held the craft and wisdom of a harpy.

"I—" and "I—" came other voices, and the women gathered around. "What do you need, good Milo?"

"Open three chambers behind the council hall. In each must be a fettering ring. Make speed. Go!"

The women ran, and Milo made his capture more complete. Flinging the three men down, breathless and numbed from his grasp, he swiftly clapped leg-irons on them one after the other, then stood up, holding the long chains together in one huge fist until the women cried out that the chambers were ready.

The bruised and subdued yachtsmen were placed in their separate cells, fettered to great iron rings, and left to cogitate over their probable fate. They were not even permitted the solace of intercourse; but as each grew more accustomed to the gloom inside, he discerned that it was no part of the plan to permit him to hunger or thirst, for a subtle gleam of ruby light shot into each small room from an unseen source, intensifying gradually and touched with its infernal radiance a small tabouret on which stood a silver flagon and a dish of the same metal containing meat.

Milo went to the great chamber in the Cave of Terrible Things when the doors had closed on his prisoners, and presented himself to Dolores. He found Pascherette prostrate on the floor before the queen, whimpering and sobbing with terror. Over her Dolores stood like Wrath in person, her beautiful face distorted with passion, fire blazing in her eyes, her breast heaving tumultuously. In her hand she held a cat-o'-nine-tails—a dainty, vicious, splendid instrument of terror—formed of plaited human hair of as many shades as thongs, studded with nuggets of gold instead

51

of lead—and none the less terrible for that—set in a cunningly carved handle of ivory. And as Milo entered, she held the whip aloft in a quivering hand, and cried to Pascherette:

"Speak, or I flay thee, traitor! What wert telling the villain, Sancho?"

Pascherette whined and cringed; she could not, or would not speak. The whip quivered, was about to fall on those dainty bare shoulders, when Milo, uttering a choking cry, flung himself forward and took the blow on his face. Dolores started back, a thing of fury, as Milo cast himself at her feet, his head on the ground, and said with submission:

"Spare the child, Sultana. Let my back bear her penance. She is faithful to thee."

Dolores halted an instant between redoubled rage and mercy; then she flung down the whip with a hard laugh, seated herself in the great chair, and bade Milo and the girl rise and come to her.

"Milo, thou'rt a fool!" she said. "Were thy brain as great as thy great heart the world might well be thine. I tell thee, child or no child, that chit is woman enough to have bound thee her slave. She is woman enough, too, to hold secret converse with my foes. Do thou speak to her now and learn for me what traffic she had with Sancho the morning after I took her as my handmaid. I give thee scant time; if I learn it not swiftly neither thou nor she shall leave this chamber alive!"

With her giant beside her, Pascherette's fears subsided in part. She peered up at him shyly and stepped closer to him, as if to seek actual shelter from the storm that threatened her; but her frightened, dependent demeanor was scarcely in accord with the new light that glinted in her sharp eyes when she dropped them from his face again. There was cunning and craft in them; the brazen assurance of a thief whose conviction is prevented by a lucky mishap.

She spoke rapidly, for his ears only, and her face drooped in an access of confusion that, beautifully simulated, satisfied Milo and sent a warm thrill into his honest breast.

"Pascherette says she only gave Sancho his answer," Milo told Dolores. "He had demanded her for his mate."

"A pretty tale!" cried Dolores impatiently. "If that be all, why so fearful of telling me, girl? Why did Sancho, who well knows the price, join Rufe against me?"

"I was afraid," murmured Pascherette with a pretty shiver. She summoned a rosy blush to her piquant face and added in a still lower whisper: "Thy anger terrified me, Sultana. My tongue was tied. And Sancho did what he did in rage, in jealousy against Milo."

The giant drew himself more erect, and his face became transfigured. If in his great heart there remained any room after his devotion to his mistress, cunning little Pascherette occupied it all when she uttered the half-admission that Milo was her man.Dolores regarded the pair silently; her expression changed slowly from irritation to query; from unbelief to amusement, and after a moment's reflection she smiled without softness and said:

"Milo, I would do much for thee. For double dealing I have no mercy. If thy love-bird would have me believe, if she is ought to thee, bid her seek Sancho and bring him to me. Let her bring him at her own hands before my hunters run him to earth, and I forgive thee both. She has fooled thee; she can fool Sancho."

Pascherette lighted up with something higher than hope: it was certainty; and while it made Milo happy it did not escape Dolores, whose dark-violet eyes once again became fathomless pools in which none might read her thoughts. She waved them from her presence, and they went out together, leaving her sitting motionless until the hangings fell behind them. Then she sprang up, ran to a great mirror, and stood for many moments regarding her lovely reflection.

"Yes, thou art beautiful!" she apostrophised. "Beautiful as an artist's dream. And for what? To queen it over these beasts! To be called Sultana, and to be in truth a caged eagle. Of them all, who save loyal Milo may I trust? Of them all, where is one whose blood mixed with mine could produce aught but devils! Yet I must slink away in the night like a whipped cur, or leave behind these treasures which alone can secure me station in the outside world." She began to pace the great apartment, oblivious of her surroundings, conscious only of a surging rebellion against even the small necessity of biding her time. The day's happenings on the schooner had shown her clearly the explosive condition of her crew; she had no mistaken ideas that for her to load up the schooner and sail away was simple. Further, she detected in recent events a growing unrest among the band, the cause of which she had but begun to fathom. Even now, through the tapestry sounding-stone, her keenly attuned ears caught a note in the cries of returning woods parties that told her how precarious was her sway over some of the more turbulent spirits.

"Before me they cringe like the dogs they are," she muttered, halting again at the mirror. "Behind my back they snap like wolves. They shall have their lesson quickly—such a one as the boldest of them shall shriek mercy." She gazed intently into the mirror, as if she would read therein an answer to her unspoken longing; then her eyes grew dark and hard; her round, strong chin set stubbornly, and she whispered intensely: "Pah! Cattle! They shall not alter my will to seek my rightful place in the world of the white man! What avails it that in my veins runs my mother's noble blood, the red chief's fiery courage, if this nest of soulless brutes is to witness my life and my end? Among those three white men is one who shall release me. They—ah, they are of a whiter, cleaner mold! Theirs is the blood that matches mine! Let them show me which is the stronger. He shall mate with me, and I will make him a king indeed, even in his own land."

Dolores stepped back panting. Then she controlled herself and began to put on garment after garment, jewel after jewel, all of superlative magnificence. Every moment she glided to the great mirror; as often she tore off a garment or a jewel, flung it down impatiently, and seized others from her boundless store. At last she stood clad like a fabled daughter of old Bagdad; a robe of shimmering silk reached her ankles, outlining every grace of her splendid figure; upon her head she had set a tiara, priceless with gems whose fire dazzled even their wearer; on arms and fingers, ankles and toes, lustrous rings and bracelets made flashing lightning with her every movement; at her girdled waist was a dagger whose sheath could have ransomed a prince.

She stood like a statue, except for the rise and fall of her breast; her eyes glittered at her gorgeous reflection in the mirror. Then suddenly her expression changed, her lips parted in scorn, and with a savage, tigerish gesture, she tore off her splendors. She stood once more in her simple tunic of knee-length, sleeveless, beauty-revealing; and picking up her dagger with the gold cord she knotted it about her waist and again regarded herself closely.

And where before she had looked upon a gorgeous woman, royally clad, weighted with gems formed by man's art, now she gazed into the limpid, fathomless eyes of a living goddess—royally clad in her own peerless loveliness, crowned with a wealth of lustrous hair in which the gleams of gold outshone the tiara she had discarded. And her face lighted; a delicate flush overspread her cheeks; the full, luscious red lips parted in a veritable Cupid's bow; and she laughed a rippling, heart-warming laugh that brought the small, even teeth glistening into view.

Dolores was satisfied at last. Without further hesitation she hurried along to the rear of the chamber and emerged into the Grove of Mysteries by way of a door known only to herself and Milo. From there she made her way silently and darkly toward the council hall.

54

CHAPTER X.

A REED SHAKEN BY THE WINDS OF PASSION.

Rupert Venner sat on the floor of his prison, tugging at his chains with an absent, aimless, all but perpetual motion; for he had long since convinced himself that his fetters could not be broken or loosed. The ruby light that had shown him the food and wine placed for him had faded away to the faintest red glow which scarcely sufficed to reach the tabouret. That mattered little; Venner had eaten when he was hungry, drunk when dry, and knew the position of the flagon and dish to the ultimate inch. He was not caring about the light. His mind was filled to the exclusion of all else with his plight and the predicament of his schooner.

"Confound me for a fool!" he mused aloud, gritting his teeth savagely. "Led by the nose by a saucy little chit who knows how to display her charms as well as her pearls!"

He pondered over his situation with growing irritation; for he knew only too well that his release could never be obtained by bribery; his keen sense of values told him that neither in the yacht or at home could he match the treasures he had already seen on the persons of Dolores, and Pascherette, and the other women of the camp. Yet he tried to console himself that after all these things might be displayed for his impression; might in fact be the entire store of the pirate queen, displayed for one gaudy, overpowering effect.

"That's it!" he cried, striking fist to palm. "Just a theatrical trick. That little jade, Pascherette, will sell her dark little soul for diamonds or pearls, I'll wager, and she shall sell me liberty. Then I'll see the queen creature, gaining entry by the same medium, and we shall see if cultivated wits are not a match for this wild beauty."

With something very like a smile of resignation Venner stretched himself on the floor and composed himself to rest. He was quite certain that Pascherette could be reached through his jailer, whoever that might be—Milo or somebody else—and the entire plan seemed to him beautifully simple and infallible. He dozed, awoke, dozed again, and the ruby light seemed to intensify each time his eyes opened.

Gradually the shaft of light grew so strong that, focused on his closed eyes, it forced him to full wakefulness; and now he stared hard at it, blinking, hypnotized by the trembling radiance that seemed to shoot out from the main shaft until a great moving circle of light appeared before him. And out from the midst of the light stepped Dolores, bewitching, irresistible, smiling down upon him with a tenderness that filled him with awe.

Amazed, dazzled, the man sat up, quivering with a sensation that rippled at his hair-roots and sent the blood singing to finger and toe-tips. And Dolores, with one forefinger at her scarlet lips to enjoin silence, glided toward him with her inimitable grace, and knelt before him shaking her head and starting him on the way to intoxication with the touch of her wonderful hair.

"My friend, I grieve that thou art here," she said, and her glowing eyes thrilled him afresh. "Wilt thou believe that it is necessary for a while?"

"Necessary?" repeated Venner, dazedly. He strove hard to burst into angry protest, but his tongue refused to utter the harsh words in the face of such a creature of beauty. "I don't understand why it isnecessary at all, lady. It is no choice of mine, or my friends, that our schooner is aground and we are your prisoners!"

"Ah, my friend, thou shalt understand," she answered, and laid a hand on his shoulder, making his senses swim with the fragrance of her breath. "But this is for thy ears alone. Thou wilt respect my confidence?" Venner nodded, wondering if, after all, the adventure might not turn out well. With Dolores so close to him that he could hear her tunic rustling to her deep, even breathing, that her loosened hair continually brushed his face, he would have nodded assent had she offered him a piece of charcoal for his immortal soul. "Then listen, man of my own people. A longing gnaws at my heart—this heart that beats under thy hand"—she took his hand with a swift movement and pressed it to her breast—"a longing to go far from this place and these brutish people, to thy land and the land to which I belong.

"And now must I say why thy ship is here? It is because I have chosen thee, my friend, to free me from this detestable bondage." She paused for a breath, leaning closer to him, then asked with a sudden grip of his hand at her breast: "Wilt take me out into thy world?"

Venner shifted uneasily beneath her blazing eyes. His soul was in torment with the touch of her; yet somewhere back of his trained brain lingered a spark of wit not yet extinguished along with his other wits by her spell. He lowered his gaze and said:

"Was there need to murder my crew, wreck my vessel, and fling me and my friends into these cells? Could not you, who are queen here, board my schooner

56

yourself and ask a passage?"

"The murder of thy crew was not of my seeking. And thinkest thou I would go from here leaving behind my treasures? Or dost fancy my rascals would permit me to carry them away? No, friend, it is not so simple. The man who aids me to attain my desire must be strong and wise and true. He shall mate with me, and my treasures shall be his. That is why I have chosen thee."

"That requires thought, lady," returned Venner, half-heartedly. "I would assist you in getting free from this, since you wish it; but as for mating or marriage, why, there is a woman at home waiting for me."

"Woman!" Dolores cried with scorn. "Woman! I am Dolores!" She swayed toward him, her arms went about his neck, and slowly, slowly her glorious eyes fastened on his, her moist, warm lips sought his in a kiss that dragged at his soul's foundations.

"Canst refuse me?" she laughed softly, drawing back her head and peering at him from under lowered lids. "See, I trust thee utterly!" Snatching her dagger from the sheath she placed it in his right hand; then, with a key from her girdle, she unfastened his chains and swayed back, still kneeling. She clutched the single shoulder-strap of her tunic, tore it from her bosom, and flung both arms wide apart. "See!" she whispered, and Rupert Venner flung away the dagger, stumbled to his feet, and swept her into his crushing embrace while she abandoned herself to him with a long, quivering sigh.

"By the gods!" he swore hoarsely, "show me what I have to do. Wonderful, wonderful Dolores!"

"Patience," she smiled, resting her head on his breast. "First tell me thy name. What shall thy Dolores call thee?"

"I am Rupert. Call me slave!"

"Rupert. It is a name to love. Slave? Nay, it is I who shall be slave to thee. But patience again, Rupert. When we two go from here, there can be no other to share our secret; none save the slaves that I shall place in thy ship to replace thy dead crew. Thy friends may not go. They must not live to see thee go!"

Venner shivered, and drew back, holding her at arms' length and staring at her in horror.

"What are you saying, Dolores?" he gasped. "My friends are to die?"

"Yes, and by thy hand, my Rupert. For how else may I know thou are worthy to be mate to a queen?"

"Now, by Heaven! Witch, siren, whatever you are, my madness has passed!" he cried. "Not for the key to a paradise peopled with such as you would I do this!" He stepped aside, picked up her dagger, and glared at her with steely eyes.

Dolores laughed at him: a low, throaty little laugh that went clear to his brain and set it on fire again. Yet, nerving himself against her, he stood erect, dagger in hand, and met the blaze of her dusky eyes bravely. He shivered violently when her rich voice thrilled his tingling ears.

"Hah, my Rupert, thou'rt not yet tamed. Let me show thee thy master!"

With the words she reached him with her subtle, tigerish glide, swiftly, startlingly, and with the dart of a cobra her hand gripped his which held the dagger. Her warm body again pressed closely to him, her red lips, parted still, almost touched his cheek; her hair smothered him with its fragrance; and while his senses swam her supple muscles tensed to living steel wire, her grip tightened and twisted at his wrist, and the dagger was wrenched from his fingers. Then leaping back, laughing mockingly now, Dolores slipped the dagger into the sheath, snatched up the chains from the floor, and flew upon him with a deadly pounce that bore him back to the wall.

Aroused from his numbness, Rupert Venner fought back furiously, humiliated, and ashamed. Whether he would or not, he forgot all his chivalry, and strove to meet this appalling woman with strength against strength; but in Dolores he met a thing of wire and whipcord where moments before had been a creature of warm softnesses; a being of feline agility, and devilish skill that reflected the devilish skill of her teacher, Milo. The chain-links tinkled and clashed against their swaying bodies, but she never let them fall; they hung from her girdle; her hands were free; and she had both his wrists in a grip that outrivaled the irons. Laughing, ever laughing, her hot breath playing over his face, she placed one foot behind one of his, surged toward him heavily, and, when his arms would have involuntarily gone out to preserve his footing, she subtly twisted them back and up from the elbows, until she rested against his chest with her bare arms tightly about his body.

Now her head, with the gold circlet about the brows, pressed hard against his chin. Her hair was in his mouth, tendrils of it stung his eyes, but the gold band numbed his flesh and bruised the bone. Upward, ever upward, she forced his chin until his neck was cracking with the strain and he choked for breath. Then she suddenly relaxed. Her arms left him, her wickedly lovely face once more smiled into his starting eyes, and she took the chain from her girdle with leisurely swiftness, falling to her knees at his feet.

"There, my friend, thou art back in thy place!" she said, snapping on his ankle irons. "Spend the night in thought, good Rupert. To-morrow I shall come to thee again for thy decision. Now, pleasant dreams, my—lover!" she whispered, suddenly slipping her arms about his neck again and pulling his head hard against her panting breast. She softly kissed his hair, then pressed back his head and kissed his lips long and passionately.

"Good night, beloved!" she said, and passed out of the room, leaving behind the echoes of a rippling little laugh that set Venner's blood to leaping.

CHAPTER XI.

PASCHERETTE UNVEILS HER PURPOSE.

Milo and Pascherette stood outside the rock portals of the great chamber after their dismissal by Dolores, and the giant's face wore a look of perplexity which was not reflected in the little octoroon. If her task was difficult, Pascherette seemed not in the least disturbed; rather in her sharp eyes lurked something of bravado at having escaped her mistress's anger so easily. And this expression perplexed Milo.

"Art sure of thyself, Pascherette?" asked the giant, ill at ease for his little companion.

"Why not?" she laughed, peering up at his troubled face impudently. "Thinkest thou Pascherette is a fool?"

"No, thou art not a fool," replied Milo slowly. He laid a heavy hand on her shoulder, turned her around to face the faint light remaining, and gazed hard into her bright eyes. "Thou art not a fool, little one. But Sancho—is it so simple to find him?"

"Big, childish Milo!" she cried with a laugh that had no joy in it. "Dost think I feared that verdict of Dolores? No. I fear her whip only. My flesh creeps even now at thought of my poor shoulders hadst thou not appeared in time. Sancho? Pah! I can find him easily enough."

"Then, child, was there nothing in thy traffic with him save what I heard from thy lips?"

Pascherette looked down, tapping the sand with her tiny foot, and her breast fluttered in agitation. Then she slipped her hand into his, looked up shyly yet ardently into his eyes, and replied swift and low:

"Milo, my love for thee must be my defense. I did have traffic with Sancho, to the end that we—thee and me—might use him to our advantage. Wait!" she cried, when he would have spoken, "hear me. Canst not see Dolores's cunning intention? She goes from here, carrying her treasure; what will she do with thee, once safely away? Will she carry thee always with her, to be marked because of thy great stature? No, Milo, thy life will pay for her desertion of her people, and she will laugh at thy passing. And why should it be? Here, thou and I can rule these cattle as she never could. With Sancho's deserters, and Rufe's followers, I can give thee a band that will force the treasure from her greedy grasp, and make of her what she has made of thee and me—a slave!"

"Girl!" Milo's deep voice vibrated with passionate horror. "Cease thy treason, or I crush thy wicked heart in these two hands. Dolores is mistress of my soul—my body is but the slave of that."

"Pish!" retorted Pascherette, contemptuously. "She has thee dazzled, Milo. Say, dost thou not love me?" she demanded, standing tiptoe and thrusting her piquant little face under his gaze. "Look in my eyes, and then tell me another woman owns thy soul!"

"Yes, I love thee," replied Milo, with simple earnestness. "I love thee; yet will I kill thee ere Dolores suffers ill through thy scheming. Have done with this talk. I hate thee for it!"

"Love—and hate!" she laughed metallically. "Loving me, still thou hast room to love another better. Hate and love! Thou great fool, it cannot be!"

"Pascherette, I love thee. Thou'rt entangled in my heart-strings. When I hate thee, it is because of that love, which will not brook treason in thee. Again, I love thee, golden girl; but, forget it not, I worship Dolores as I worship my gods!"

"Then wilt thou not seek her power for thyself?" whispered the girl subduedly, awed for the moment by his tremendous and solemn earnestness.

"Little one, bring Sancho as she bade thee. He has merited punishment. Yet tell him the Sultana will be just. His punishment will but fit the fault. Afterward we two will talk together, and I shall teach thee loyalty. Go now, bring thy man to the council hall. I shall await thee. Stay, I shall come with thee, for the woods are dark, and a storm threatens."

"I go alone, Milo. He will fly from thee. Have no fear for me; the woods are safe, and the storm is in thy great head only."

The girl turned, kissed her hand airily, and ran into the gloom of the forest. And as she went she laughed again harshly and muttered: "The great clod! His worship overtops his love. But I shall make love overtop worship yet, my giant! Such a man—a slave? Not for a thousand Doloreses! Wait, Milo; wait, my mistress!"

The evening breeze had strengthened as darkness fell, and its breath was hot and sultry. As Pascherette plunged deeper into the woods, the heavy boom of the seas along shore died away and gave place to the softer, more vibrant hum and murmur of the great trees. The track, little more than a line of flattened underbrush, vanished before she had gone fifty yards; but the little octoroon was no stranger to nocturnal rambles, her keen eyes, and, keener still, her sense of direction, led her unerringly through the shades toward the rearward spur of the granite cliff. Creepers and hanging mosses brushed her face and limbs; alone she might have ignored them; but there was a quality in the sighing and rustling about her that seemed to give voices to the ghostly fingers that touchedher, and to support her courage as well as to warn Sancho of her coming, she thrilled forth a merry little snatch of song:

"Ho! for the Jolly Roger lads;
Ho! for the decks red-streaming.
A pirate's lass is a well-lov'd lass,
And there's gold through the red a gleaming!

"Ho! for a cask in the fire's red glow;
Ho! for the heaps of plunder.
There are showers of pearls for the pirates' girls—
The rain from the corsair's thunder!"

At the end of her song Pascherette halted, listened, then called softly:
"Sancho! Thy Pascherette calls!"
Silence prevailed for several moments, and she called again, fearing that her voice had gone astray amid the increasing confusion of the trees. Then came a lull in the wind, the lull that always punctuated the gathering of such tropical storms as now threatened; and in the hush she heard voices—uncertain, disputing. Then Sancho growled, close to her ear:
"Art alone, jade?"
"Oh, Sancho!" she cried, darting into the gloom to the sound of his voice and flinging her arms about him. "I have feared for thee, my Sancho. Now I fear no more, for all is well."
"Well?" the pirate growled suspiciously. "Hast left thy hot-blood mistress, then?"
"No, Sancho. It is better for thee even than that. I have made thy peace with Dolores. She has forgiven thee, and wishes to tell thee so."
A fervid curse burst from some one yet invisible, and Sancho leaned back to catch some whispered words. Then he, too, ripped out an oath, and gripped Pascherette tightly by the arm.

62

"This is a trick, little devil! Don't you value that pretty little head more than to trifle with me?"

"I trifle with thee? Thou art mad, Sancho!" she cried. "Did I lie when I said I loved thee, then?"

"The fiend knows! I know 'tis plaguey risky for thee if thou didst!"

"Unbeliever!" whispered Pascherette with thrilling emphasis. "Shall I tell thee again, in language even thy stubborn soul must believe?"

The girl suddenly glided inside his arms, flung up her hands, each clutching a mass of her glossy, scented hair, and enmeshed his disfigured face. Then, straining upward from her small height, her rosy, false lips sought his and fastened there while he staggered as if drunk.

"There, heart o' mine!" she panted. "Dost believe now? Or must I tell thee again that with such love as mine proud Dolores cannot hurt thee. Come! Such a chance will never come thy way again. Man! 'Tis her confidence Dolores offers thee. Shall it go begging because of thy madness?"

"Pascherette!" returned Sancho hoarsely. "I will go with thee. But, girl, thy heart's blood pours at first sign of treachery! Mark that well. And tell me now, does Yellow Rufe share in this mercy?"

"No, Sancho. It cannot be. Dolores has sworn to hunt him down; the woods are full of men even now, seeking him and thee. Only by going with me wilt thou escape them and have advantage from my pleading with the queen." She drew his head down to her ear, and whispered rapidly. Doubt, then admiration, crept into Sancho's voice as he said: "Dost think it can be done? Can he gain the sloop unseen?"

"I will make it easy, Sancho. Bid Rufe have no fear. The storm will be upon us within an hour. It is dark; there is wind aplenty. With six men he may win clear; and listen: If he is stout of heart, what is to stop him taking tribute from the stranger's white vessel?"

"Lack o' powder, girl," returned Sancho angrily. "Thy mistress keeps us short of powder, as well thou dost know, lest we become too strong for her. Who of us has ever seen the store? Not I, by Satan! Canst thou get powder and shot for Rufe?"

"Simpleton! Can he not get with steel all he wants from the schooner?"

"By the heart of Portuguez, he can!" cried another voice, and Yellow Rufe strode through the bushes.

"Rufe!" exclaimed the girl, feigning astonishment. Her ears were too keen not to have caught Rufe's voice in the whispering that had gone on.

"Yes, Rufe, and obliged to thee, Pascherette. Dost say thou wilt help me win away?"

"Gladly, Rufe, for I like well men of your mettle. Follow close behind Sancho and me. Count ten score after we go in to Dolores with Milo, then for an hour thou'lt have the sea to thyself. Luck go with thee, Rufe; thou'lt think of little Pascherette sometimes, I'll warrant."

A rumble of thunder rolled up from the sea, and lightning played in the tree-tops. Pascherette turned back toward the camp, and giving no heed to Sancho save to listen for his footsteps, she ran through the darkness sure-footed, sure-eyed as a cat. Rain began to fall, and the heavy foliage thrummed with the growing down-pour which yet did not penetrate to the earth. As they neared the shore, the forest resounded with the solemn boom and crash of long-sweeping seas outside the bar; the wind screamed among the huts; all the women and those men who had returned from their portion of the search were snugly under cover. The place seemed desert-ed.

"Farewell, Rufe," Pascherette whispered at last, when the great black mass of the council hall loomed against the sky in a lightning flash. "Count ten score. Thy safety is in my hands."

Then she took Sancho by the hand, and led him through the plashing rain to the rear of the hall and called softly: "Milo!"

"Here. Hast found him?"

"Take us to the Sultana quickly, Milo. I have told Sancho to trust in the justice of Dolores."

"He may well do that," returned Milo. "The great Sultana is ever just."

"Yes, have no fear, good Sancho. I am Justice itself!" rejoined the mellow voice of Dolores in person, who had a few moments before left Rupert Venner. "Milo, I am minded to give Sancho proof of my mercy, since he already believes in my jus-tice. Open the great chamber. Sancho, canst guess the honor I propose to do thee?"

"No, lady," replied Sancho, an awful dryness gripping his throat.

"Hast ever hungered for sight of the great chamber?" She paused smiling at the uneasy pirate, who could not answer. "Of course thou hast," she replied for him. "Which of my rogues has not? I am minded to show thee this mark of my love, since thy conscience permitted thee to return here. Hast any fear of the saying the Red Chief uttered? That none might enter the great chamber and live?"

Sancho suddenly sprang to life. His face was distorted; when the lightning flashed it revealed him a ghastly picture of apprehension.

"I will not go there! I have no wish to see what my eyes are forbidden to see. I never sought to enter, Sultana. It was the others!"

"Yes, Sancho, the others. That is why I select thee for the honor, because thou wert patient. Come. I promise thee thy life is safe."

Dolores passed on toward the great stone, where Milo stood guard over the opened portals. Sancho, trembling violently, was drawn irresistibly after her, partly fascinated by her calm strength, partly influenced by the soft fingers and whispered prattle of Pascherette, who strove to set him aflame with mention of some of the wonders he was to see.

He paused at the rock door, glancing around with a vague premonition of evil; but now it was Dolores's hand that took his; Dolores's rich voice that lured him on; and he stepped after her, smothering a sob of resurging terror as the great stone fell into its place behind.

CHAPTER XII.

SANCHO SETTLES HIS ACCOUNT.

In the rock passage the hush was complete. For the space of ten long breaths San-cho stood quivering under the weird spell of the infernal red radiance from the hidden lights, while almost invisible ahead of him Dolores bent to listen to a last moment's communication from Pascherette. With Milo behind him, and the great unknown ahead, the pirate's usual fierce courage oozed out through his boots. Yet he was hypnotized by the vague glitter that shone at the end of the tunnel—the glit-ter,though he knew it not yet, of the great sliding door to the inner mystery.

Suddenly the mighty rock reverberated and shook to a Titanic volley of thunder, and Sancho shrieked with nervous terror. His shriek was echoed by a rippling laugh from Dolores, and she came back swiftly toward him, pushing Pascherette before her. She handed the little octoroon on to Milo, and said, with a kindly pat on the girl's head: "Open, Milo, and let thy sweetheart complete her good works. Now I shall have none but faithful friends about me. Pascherette, thou'rt more than for-given: thou'rt my good friend. I shall reward thee fittingly when"—she smiled daz-zlingly at Sancho—"I have rewarded Sancho."

The rock door rolled aside, and Pascherette passed out into the storm. Sancho's nerves gave way utterly now, and he rushed toward the opening, screaming: "Let me out! I want air! I want none of the great chamber! Let me pass!"

Milo again let fall the rock, pressed a huge hand on Sancho's breast, and pushed him back, saying: "Peace, fool! Go with thy mistress. Thine eye will never again witness the like. Go, I tell thee. Dost fear the Sultana's justice?"

"Come, Sancho. Thou'lt be a marked man among thy fellows when I have shown thee what they yearn to see."

Dolores again took his hand, bent her glorious eyes full upon him, and Sancho followed her like a sheep, straight to the great door under the jeweled yellow lantern, where he stood, stupefied with awe at the barbaric splendors revealed.

His lips went dry, and he licked them feverishly; his single eye blazed with avarice; the two fingers and mutilated thumb of his right hand worked convulsively, as if he would tear the gems and plate from the door. And Dolores watched him from under lowered lids, her rich red lips curled scornfully, one hand half raised to warn Milo to open the great door slowly.

"Well, Sancho, art better prepared for the greater treasures yet to be seen?" smiled Dolores. The pirate's blazing eye seemed to dart flames as the door slowly rose to Milo's touch.

"Sultana!" he gasped, and his speech would do no more for him.

"Enter, friend. This is thy great hour!"

The queen pushed him gently inside, following herself, and Milo let fall the door again, standing mute and motionless on the inside while his mistress led the pirate to the center of the great chamber and waited until his dazzled eye adjusted itself to the subtle lighting effects.

Pascherette's last whispered communication to Dolores had told her of Yellow Rufe's intentions; and while Sancho stood in amaze, she bent her ear to catch the expected sound of voices through the sounding-stone behind the tapestry. For there the little octoroon was to play a part for Sancho's especial benefit. The thunder had become all but incessant; with every crash the great chamber rumbled and echoed eerily; yet between the crashes, brief as the periods were, human voices could be heard.

"Art ready to see my treasures, Sancho?"

Dolores waved a gleaming arm around the place, indicating with one wide gesture the glories of the walls and roof. But the pirate's senses responded more readily to the tangible riches represented by gold and gems, tall flagons, and jewel-incrusted lamps, littered diamonds and rubies that strewed the big table.

"Hah!" cried Dolores, with a low, throaty laugh. "Ah! my friend, I know thy mind. Milo!"

Milo advanced with a deep obeisance.

"Milo, open the great chests for Sancho. Let him plunge his arms to the elbows in red gold. Then I shall show him that which lies nearest to his deserts."

The pirate watched with lips no longer dry, but dripping with the saliva of greed, while Milo flung open chest after chest, full to overflowing with minted gold of many nations; looted jewels of royal and noble houses, sacred vessels and glittering orders, weapons whose hilts and scabbards, if ever made for use, could only have been used to bewilder the eye and senses.

Again the thunder pealed; and in the tremendous hush succeeding, the voices outside penetrated the sounding-stone in more than a whisper. Sancho jerked up his head and fear once more shone in his single eye.

"Come, good Sancho," purred Dolores, running her soft hand down his bare forearm. "Art frightened by petty noises, then? Plunge thy hands deep, man! All thou canst grasp is thine for so long as thy eye can enjoy or thy hands fondle."

Now Sancho's sordid soul surrendered. His greed conquered fear, and he delved deep into a coffer, chattering the while with frenzy. And now when the thunder rolled, his ears heard it not. He drew forth his hands, and a glittering mass of wealth fell about his feet. He glared up at Dolores, laughing ghoulishly.

"That is well, Sancho," Dolores said, and took his hand. "Now I will show thee the rest; and I know thou'lt never tell of it. I trust thee. Come. Put thy ear to this tapestry, and tell me what thou canst hear."

Sancho laid his ear to the cloth, and his eye gleamed brightly. Milo stepped silently behind him.

"I hear Hanglip!" he gasped. "Is he, too, here?"

"He is outside the cliff. But whom else canst hear?"

"I hear Caliban—Spotted Dog—Stumpy—I hear a score as if they stood by my side! And Pascherette! By the fiend! She has played Rufe a trick! And me—" He sprang from the wall like a tiger, snatching at his weaponless belt with slavering fury, to be gathered at once into the remorseless hug of Milo. And he glared full into the mocking face of Dolores—soft and generous no more, but the embodiment of awful vengeance.

For many seconds she stood regarding him contemptuously, until he subsided helplessly in Milo's grasp; then, motioning the giant to follow, she passed along and stopped before a life-size painting of "The Sleeping Venus" in a massive, gilded frame. With one hand raised high at the side, she turned a pulley-catch, and the great picture slowly fell forward from the top until it rested slopingly on the floor, forming an inclined entrance to a gloomy passage, dimly touched by a dark-red glow.

This was the secret outlet to the great chamber by which Milo had access to the altar in the grove at such times as his aid was needed to support Dolores in some exhibition of black magic. She stepped swiftly along the passage, giving no further heed to the panic-stricken pirate until Milo had carried and dragged him to where she awaited him. This was still another dark excavation, running deeper yet into the bowels of the cliff; and the devilish red glare was here intensified until surrounding objects were vividly revealed.

"Now hear the doom of a traitor!" cried Dolores, with haughty mien. "What! Not a traitor?" she mocked at the pirate's frantic howl of denial. "Then Dolores has

68

erred, perhaps. There is a test, good Sancho. Let me see if I am wrong!"

She signed to Milo, and the giant swung Sancho around until he faced the deepest recess of the cave. There, swathed in mummy clothes, preserved by the chemical miracle of the stratum of red earth that formed the core of the rock, the body of Red Jabez stood erect against the wall, bathed in the red glow, diamonds glittering where the dead eyes had been. And on the rock ledge at his feet stood a tall flagon of gold, in which Dolores had brewed an awful potion for this event. Beside this ledge stood a low brazier full of glowing charcoal; on a tabouret near by lay several terrible implements the use of which needed no explanation.

"Look upon the face of the Red Chief, and drink this draft—'tis his blood!" she cried, seizing the flagon and thrusting it into Sancho's hands. "Then, if thy heart held no treachery toward me, thy life and limbs are safe. But have a care! A lie in thy heart will surely undo thee. Drink!"

A splitting thunder-crash filled the place with uproar; a gust of the tempest from the outer entrance sent the wind swirling in. It was as if the breath of the storm snatched Sancho's senses back from the terror-land they had fled to; he ceased his howling, glared defiantly up at the dead chief, and cried in desperation: "Give me the drink! I fear neither gods nor devils; why should I fear you, dead man?"

"Wait!" Dolores laid a hand on his arm, and stayed the flagon at his lips. "Wait, till I tell thee more. Then, if thou art guiltless, and go from here with the treasure I gave thee, thou'lt know thy friends and thy foes.

"Didst think Yellow Rufe was free? Thou fool! Thy wits are powerless before a woman's. Did my pretty Pascherette tell him he might go free, taking my sloop, escaping my vengeance, as thou didst think to? Didst hear those voices? Then I tell thee, Sancho, that ten-score count, that Rufe doubtless made in fear and trembling, but sufficed to raise his hopes. For ere he had gained the sloop and started her anchor, Pascherette had done her work. The stranger's schooner is full of my men, waiting for Rufe to come for his booty. Let him take alarm, then how far may he win? Thou'lt never know, false Sancho, for I have no doubt of thy treachery. Now drink, if thou darest!"

"Then, by the fiend, I dare!" shouted the pirate. Something in the tang of the gale sweeping in from the unseen entrance reassured him of the existence of the outer world; persuaded him that by taking a desperate chance he might yet throw dust in the eyes of this terrible woman and go hence with the secret of the great chamber. "I dare, Dolores! Blood, d' ye say? What fitter drink for a pirate?"

He lifted the flagon, took a deep draft in great gulps, so that his determination might carry him; then his eye sparkled, he took the flagon from his lips, and grinned at Milo. "By the great Red Chief!" he cried. "This is justice indeed! I drink to ye, Sultana, and to Milo, ye big jester!" and finished the drink with a greedy swallow.

Then the flagon clattered to the ground, Sancho's face went livid, and his mouth opened wide and loosely, as his body and limbs were seized with subtle pains. His brain, too, felt an awful numbness creeping upon it; for the draft had done its work. The rarest of wine from her store, Dolores had mingled with it a devilish powder that first sapped the strength, then attacked the brain, and eventually snapped the cord of intelligence, leaving the victim a driveling imbecile. But that point had not yet been reached. It would come perhaps in one hour, two, three, perhaps six—but inevitably it must come. For the present the pirate was simply in the grip of the un-known, yet having full power to realize, but not resist, the tangible terrors at hand.

"Milo, hasten the rest. I shall await thee at the gate. Put forth this traitor by the Grove outlet, and see to it that he takes with him neither power to see beauty, to utter treason, or to ever feel again the scalding touch of coveted gold. Make speed, I command thee, for I hear my stout trusty ones clamoring for the chase!"

Dolores disappeared through the secret outlet, sprang down behind the altar, and ran through the Grove. Beside the cliff were huddled Hanglip and Stumpy, Caliban, and Spotted Dog, drenched with the teeming rain, restless with impa-tience, peering ever to seaward in the lightning flashes that continually illumined the scene.

Among them Dolores appeared, suddenly, mysteriously, as coming from the skies, and after a choke of amazement Stumpy flung a hand seaward, and shouted above the turmoil of wind and rain:

"Queen o' Night, thou'lt need thy magic now! See, there flies the villain!"

Dolores looked, and smiled disdainfully. The torrential rain beat upon her bare head and shoulders, causing her to glisten and shine like a golden goddess; but she heeded it not at all; her eyes sought out what Stumpy had indicated. And there, in the next lightning-flash, flying seaward, was the sloop. Rufe had taken alarm, and had foregone his plan of looting the schooner.

"Let him go; he'll fly not far," she said calmly. "Come with me to the great rock, my bold fellows; daylight shall show thee Rufe where I would have him—paying the price, as Sancho has paid!"

She glided around the rock, followed by her silent faithfuls, while from the Grove rang a shriek of mortal agony that sent fierce hearts aquiver with terror.

70

CHAPTER XIII.

DOLORES FLOATS THE FEU FOLLETTE.

"Hell's breath!" screamed Caliban, as the cry rang out. "Have ye devils in the Grove, mistress?" Hanglip and Spotted Dog, too, cringedback in fright. Stumpy concealed his uneasiness, yet his eyes searched Dolores's face questingly. None truly believed in the queen's magic powers; yet none was bold enough to openly avow his unbelief; and the added grimness of the storm, assisted by the unearthliness of that howl of anguish, brought the four godless pirates to the verge of superstitious terror.

"Yes, I keep my devils there," replied Dolores; "and that is the traitor Sancho answering to them for his perfidy. So watch, and obey me, lest thy cries, too, go up from my altar!"

She stood apart at the great stone, listening, and presently Milo rolled up the rock barrier, and appeared in the gloom, calm and cool as if he had no association with devils, imaginary or otherwise. A livid lightning-flash played on his features, and the pirates drew back, muttering at his black eyes which glowed with red points like rubies in the heart of twin coals.

"Milo, there flies Rufe," said Dolores, flinging an arm seaward. Beyond the false point, in the midst of black seas dappled with rushing white-horses, under a lowering black sky that seemed to lean down to the verge of the ocean itself, Rufe's sloop was pictured in the next flash of electric radiance a thing of desolation and panic. Fully a mile away, the craft vanished in the pervading blackness between every flash. "I need thy condor's vision now as never before. Take the swift, small sailboat, and flares; follow the sloop as long as thy eyes can pick her out; we shall follow thy flares in the schooner until we overtake thee. Haste now; Rufe has grace enough!"

Milo stayed only to get his flare-powder and tinder-box, then disappeared down the cliff.

Dolores despatched her four attendants to the schooner, prepared to follow, then, with an afterthought, halted two of them.

"Here, Hanglip, Spotted Dog, wait!" She swiftly entered the council hall, went to the three small chambers, and released her captives from the ring-bolts. Driving them before her, bewildered by the sudden emergence from tranquillity to the turmoil of the storm, she gave the two pirates each a chain, held the other herself, and led the way down to the stranded schooner. Her motive was not only uncertainty about the people left at the camp, who might prove susceptible to bribery if not pity; she also felt a sort of whimsical desire to impress these strangers with the utter inevitability of her power.

The Feu Follette lay on the edge of the bar, as she had lain since stranding, except that with tide after tide her keel had worn itself a place in the sand, and she was less closely held than before. Of her rightful crew but five survived the fight; one was the sailing-master, Peters, and all were imprisoned under jailers in the forecastle. On the schooner's sloping decks, when Dolores and her party climbed aboard, were a score of nondescript pirates, besides the crew's custodians, at a loss to account for the escape of the sloop, and worked up to a pitch of nervousness where they were only fit for sudden, strenuous action with a merciless taskmaster. And such they speedily had.

Dolores ordered her three captives to be taken to the great cabin, and their chains were fastened to the ornately paneled mainmast which ran down through both decks and formed the support of a gorgeously furnished sideboard. Then the companionway was locked on them, and the girl sprang to tremendous life.

"Aloft with thee, Stumpy!" she cried, selecting him because after Milo his eyes were keenest of them all. "Keep thy eyes open for Milo's flares, and mark well the direction. Hanglip, thou surly dog! Take ten men and lay me out a good anchor astern, with a stout hawser. Be brisk! Come aboard in ten minutes, or thy back shall smart."

Sancho's boat had remained at the port quarter, and into this Hanglip drove his crew while Spotted Dog with the rest of the men got ready an anchor to lower to them.

"Caliban, cast off the gaskets from fore and main!" cried Dolores next. "Where are thy rascals? Plague take thee, hunchback! Couldst not say there were not men enough? Below with ye, and bring up the schooner's people. Have sail on this vesselbefore that anchor takes hold, or I'll flay thy hump!"

Cursing venomously, the deformed little demon sprang into the forecastle and drove up Peters and his four men with kicks and blows. They, too, were bewildered by the tremendous uproar of sea and wind, and went like sheep to the fore and main masts at Caliban's bidding.

"Ready for the anchor—lower away!" roared Hanglip in the boat, where already was piled coil on coil a great hemp hawser.

"Handsomely, ye dogs, handsomely!" shrieked Spotted Dog in turn. The anchor sank into the boat to the screeching of tackles and the groaning of boat-timbers, and was carried out astern.

"Carry the end aft!" Dolores commanded; the hawser was taken along and the end passed around the quarter-deck capstan. "Up with those sails!" cried the girl now, and Caliban's gang sweated at the halyards, while slackened sheets permitted the booms to swing and present the luffs to the screaming gale, bearing no resistance. While the boat pulled away into the darkness astern, carrying the anchor to the full scope of the cable, Dolores kept her eyes ever aloft, and over the sea, and upon every detail of the work. Her eyes fell upon Peters, standing in sullen mood at the belaying-pin which held a turn of the main-throat halyards. And as the croaking cry of Caliban ordered "Belay!" she called Peters to her.

"Thou'rt sailing-master, hey?"

"I was."

"Art still, if thy heart is as stubborn as thy face!" cried Dolores, laughing at his scowl. "Canst sail thy ship now?"

"I can sail any ship that floats, but neither I nor your sharks can sail this schooner now," he replied surlily. "Your false marks did their work well."

"Then thou'd rather pull a rope than hold a wheel, hey? 'Tis but a wooden sailor, after all. I hoped such a ship would boast a seaman as master. I'll show thee seamanship, sheep-heart!"

Out of the darkness astern came a roar:

"Anchor's down! Heave away!"

And from the darkness aloft Stumpy bawled:

"There she flares! Mother o' me!" The prayer, curse, whatever the last words might be, were called forth by a paralyzing flash of lightning that shone over the raging sea like a gigantic calcium-light. The schooner's deck resounded with superstitious howls, which rose to awed cries from the weakest as from trucks and gaff-ends glowed and flickered the blue brush of St. Elmo's fire.

"Heave away, heave away!" Dolores's voice rang out on the hubbub, forcing obedience even in face of terror. The capstan went round to the urge of a dozen pair of fear-stimulated arms; and fathom by fathom the great cable came in dripping and glistening; fathom after fathom was heaped on the deck, and still the schooner remained fast. And ever from aloft came Stumpy's hail, reporting Milo's flare fast fading in the distance.

"You can't do it! I knew it!" shouted Peters defiantly.

"Peace, sheep!" answered Dolores, slapping him upon the mouth. She stood at the wheel, and no part of the vessel's situation escaped her. She had yet a trump to play: a hazardous one, truly, but the big one. The big fore and main sails swung and crashed idly at their sheets, filling the air with the thunder of their flinging blocks. At each boom a seaman stood, and each held the double block of a boom-tackle, waiting the word that now came.

"Clap on those boom-tackles!" Dolores commanded, and four men flew to each as it was hooked to the rigging. "Haul away! Boom the sails square out!" The great sails filled with a crash as the gale took them on the fore side, flinging them violently aback.

"You'll pluck the spars out of her!" screamed Peters, in a frenzy now as his cherished masts whipped and cracked to the tremendous backward strain. Dolores ignored the crazed man, but a scornful smile wreathed about her lips, and her dark eyes gleamed. "Out with them!" she cried. "More hands there! And heave, ho, heave away on the capstan! Burst thy arms, bullies! Here comes Hanglip and his bold lads to help ye! Round with her! Out with them! Heave, good bullies!"

The girl stood by the wheel, a splendid figure of matchless energy and courage.Aloft the topmasts bent like whips; Stumpy's voice came down in ever-increasing fear as his perch grew shakier; the great expanse of canvas, which should have been treble-reefed even in a floating ship going forward, tore at boom-tackles and earrings, tacks, and mast-hoops, shaking the vessel to the keel and filling her with cataclysmic thunder.

"By the bones of Red Jabez, she comes!" roared Spotted Dog, peering over the side. "Heave, lads, and never doubt the girl again! Fiends o' Topheth! See her slide!"

The schooner shuddered from forefoot to sternpost; the big hawser slipped in through the lead with gathering speed; the groaning masts imparted an impulse to her that drove her astern like an arrow, and now, triumphantly, Dolores cried:

"An ax! Quickly—cut the hawser! Caliban, get a jib loosed! Hanglip, open the companionway, and bring up my prisoners. I would have them enjoy the sail."

A curling sea poured over the taffrail, sweeping Dolores from her feet; she met it with a ringing laugh, gripping the wheel as her safeguard, and the moment the ax severed the hawser she gave the vessel a sheer with the helm, and again her orders rang out:

"Let go both boom-tackles! Hoist away the jib! Haul the jib-sheet to starboard,

74

and stand by fore and main sheets!"

Out of the darkness ahead came the fluttering of canvas, and soon Caliban's hoarse croak rang aft: "Hoist away th' jib!" The great booms swung amidships again when the tackles were cast off, and now the headsail flew up the stay, the re-strained sheet to starboard causing the canvas to fill aback as had the greater sails before. The pressure was ahead and to one side; the schooner's head began to fall off, then faster as she gained momentum, and the fore and main sails again began to thunder at their blocks.

"Let draw the jib! Bring in the fore sheet; bear a hand aft here, main sheet, lads, smartly!" cried Dolores, twirling the wheel to meet the vessel's swift leeward leap. And as the liberated Feu Follette heeled dizzily to the gale, under full spread of sail, and her owner and his guests appeared into the storm, Stumpy's cry rang out:

CHAPTER XIV.

YELLOW RUFE'S FINISH.

"How bears the flare?" Dolores demanded, steadying the helm.

"Three points on lee-bow!" came from aloft.

"Sing out when we point for it!" Dolores gave the wheel a few spokes, and at her command the main-sheet was rendered until the schooner fell off from the wind, and Stumpy hailed: "Steady! She heads fair for it!"

"Does it still burn?"

"Aye, blazing bright! And low down, too, for the seas hide it every moment!"

"Keep thy eyes skinned, and seek for the sloop, too."

The schooner came to a more even keel as she squared away from the gale, and the splendid speed of the craft sent a thrill through Dolores, as through the less impressionable pirate of the gang. Fast as Rufe's sloop was, this dainty plaything of wealth and leisure sped over the snarling seas at a gait that promised to overhaul the smaller vessel two fathoms to one.

Even Rupert Venner and his friends, shivering with the wet and sudden change from the cabin to the deck though they were, found much to soothe them in the glorious sweep and swing of the Feu Follette; much to admire and envy in the perfect poise and sang froid of the magnificent creature at the wheel.

Dolores stood on feet as steady as the great, deep eyes that were fixed on the compass-card before her. Her heavy, lustrous hair streamed about her from under the golden circlet; in each lightning flash she stood out, a thing of wild, awful beauty; the rain glistened on her bare shoulders and arms, rendering her golden skin a gleaming, fairylike armor. And the blustering wind caught her wet tunic and wrapped it about her closely and tightly, revealing every grace and glory of her perfect body.

"Saints! Was there ever such a creature?" said Tomlin hoarsely.

Pearse's face was set and grim; he made no rejoinder. Venner, too, kept silent; but his eyes held venom as he glared at the speaker. Dolores suddenly raised her

76

eyes from the binnacle, looked toward them as they crouched shivering in the lee of the deck-house-companion, and she, warm and glowing in a flimsy, wet garment, laughed mockingly, and called to them.

"I am forgetting what is due to my guests. Do ye feel cold? Will ye go below?"

And they, shivering and uneasy as they were, were content to shiver if only they might not lose sight of her. Their reply was unintelligible; neither would look at the others; yet their mumbled response was understood, and the girl laughed again, loud, ringing, and full of allure.

"Such courage comes only of true sea stock, my friends! I shall not forget this fortitude when I have done with the schooner."

"Flare close aboard!" roared Stumpy; then: "Seize my soul if I see the boat, though, mistress. Satan! Now the flare's gone out!"

"Whereaway?" cried Dolores shrilly. Big Milo was out there in the blackness.

"Right under the bows!" bellowed the lookout. "Luff, or bear away; ye'll run him down!"

And from the raging seas off the lee-bow came the deep, calm voice of Milo, unperturbed as if on dry land, though no boat was to be seen in the murk. "Hold the course, Sultana, I am here!"

And on the heels of the words came a flash from the skies, blazing full upon the dripping figure of the giant as he reached a great arm up, gripped the lee-rail, and swung himself on board with the unconscious ease of a perfect athlete.

"Thy boat, Milo?" inquired Dolores.

"Sailed under, Sultana. I have held the flare aloft in my hand while swimming until a moment ago, when the powder burned out."

"And Rufe?"

"The sloop is close by. Thou art sailing fair at his stern if thy course was not changed to avoid me. His topmast is gone; he sails slowly."

Then without more ado the splendid human animal clutched a backstay and swarmed aloft with the agility of an ape, showing not a whit of strain after his battle with the roaring seas. He reached Stumpy, sent that numbed mariner down, and searched the waters with his keen vision, waiting for another lightning flash. And when it came, fainter now as the thunderstorm receded, his resonant voice boomed down:

"Broad abeam the sloop lies! She runs before the wind!"

"Slack away the main-sheet!" cried Dolores, heaving the helm up. "Hail every minute, Milo!"

"Shall I send him a shot immediately, lady?" roared Hanglip, at the schooner's foremost gun.

"Hold with thy shots, villain! Does Rufe deserve no sport? Stand by with the grappling-hooks. I'll run him down!"

"The sloop is dead ahead!" hailed Milo, though none on deck could detect anything of her in the blackness. Dolores listened intently; then twirled the wheel, and cried: "I hear her! Ready the grapnels?"

"Aye, ready!"

"Then watch—and heave!" she commanded; and with the suddenness of light the schooner swept around in a swift arc, the black shape of the flying sloop stood out against the angry sea crests, and the two vessels came together with a crash of timbers and a rattling of gear.

A distant rumbling of thunder succeeded a faint flash, and wind and rain came down with increased fury as if to balance the defection of the electric element. The darkness of Erebus fell upon the surging vessels, and men groped at the rails in a blind effort to make out a footing for boarding the sloop.

"Follow me; I want Yellow Rufe alive!" cried Dolores, leaving the wheel and springing to the bulwarks. Instinctively Peters stepped to the wheel, and as he passed his employer he leaned to whisper in his ear:

"Let them once leave these decks, sir, and we'll up hellum and away!"

Venner's eyes glittered at the prospect; but he could not see the faces of his friends; he could only hear Pearse's low tones beside him, and the mumbled words indicated no great agreement in the scheme. Uncertain, his mind confused between desire to escape and desire to see more of Dolores and her hidden cave of wonders, Rupert Venner hesitated in his decision; and in the next moment it was out of his power to decide. For Rufe, in desperation now, met the boarders at the rail, backed by his half-dozen crazed adherents, and murderous steel glittered dully against the inky sky.

"Beat down his cringing curs, but leave me Rufe!" cried Dolores, opposing her own dagger to the sweep of the pirate's cutlas. And as the schooner's crew roared at Hanglip's heels, storming over to the pitching sloop's decks to pursue mercilessly the panic-stricken runaways, the girl pitted agility and splendid knife-craft against the terror-driven strength and wolfish fury of the trapped traitor.

"Hah! Thy black heart fails thee!" taunted Dolores, leaping down from the rail to the schooner's streaming deck and thus avoiding a whistling stroke of Rufe's cutlas. The pirate fell forward with the impetus of his blow, and stumbled in a heap at the girl's nimble feet. "Up, man!" she cried, leaping back to permit him to rise. "What, art afraid of a woman? Here, then, I prick thee! Now wilt fight?" She darted her dagger swiftly downward, and the partially healed cross on Rufe's cheek blazed red again.

"Woman or devil, I'll see thy heart for that!" swore the pirate, and rose with a bound and hurled himself at the girl. She stepped aside agilely and laughed mockingly at him, while as he again stumbled with the swing of his avoided blow she darted close, and her knife ripped his sword-arm from wrist to elbow.

Mouthing crazily with fury, Rufe leaped backward until his shoulders struck the rigging, and, seizing his cutlas in his left hand, he poised it by the blade for a deadly javelin cast.

Now upon the scene flared a great blaze, and Stumpy's scowling face appeared at the back of it. He, with readier wit than his fellows, had sought out a tar-pot and lamp; and at the moment his mistress stood defenseless before the impeding steel, the club-footed pirate poured lamp-oil into the tar, and cast the flaring wick on top of all.

A circle of light spread from wheel to foremast, with Yellow Rufe at the main rigging in the center of it. The light dazzled him for a second, and his throw was stayed. The three yachtsmen, huddled in their chains aft, stared in helpless amazement at the tableau; for such it became, when the fight stopped for a breath and every man's passion-filled face was lighted by the red glare.

"Shoot him down!" shouted Pearse in horror.

And Venner and Tomlin strove for words without success. Venner was dumb and sick in face of Dolores's peril. Yellow Rufeuttered a grim, Satanic growl of laughter, and drew back his arm for the cast. His plight was utterly desperate; he knew death waited for him with clutching talons, and with his last breath he would reap toll that should make his name a thing to recall with dread afterward.

"This for thy witch's heart!" he howled, and his arm quivered. Then out of the shadows aloft, above the smoky flare, came down the tremendous shape of Milo, forgotten in his post at the masthead, but never taking his eyes from his Sultana.

Like a gorilla he slipped down the backstay with one hand; with the other hand he reached downward with a swift, sure clutch, and as Rufe's wrist flexed to cast his javelin Milo's hand gripped him by the neck from behind and swung him bodily off his feet, while the wide-flung cutlas flashed through the air and plunged with a hiss over the side.

"I thank thee again, Milo," said Dolores, slipping her dagger into the sheath and looking on at Rufe's struggles with the unconcern of one far apart from the actual conflict. "I wished to take him alive; yet had almost been forced to cut too deeply. Bring the villain to me. And, Caliban, get more flares, lanterns, lights, and make us a theater of justice here."

She stepped aft, saw Peters at the wheel, and smiled as she realized how her boarding of the sloop might have resulted.

"Hah, but it would have availed thee nothing!" she smiled at Venner. "I read thy heart as I read the stars, friend. Watch how completely Yellow Rufe pays his debt to me. He has fled me through forest and mountain; through a sea of howling storm; yet he pays. And thus all men pay who think to flout Dolores. Keep thy eyes wide, friends, and watch."

Yellow Rufe was brought before her, and his swarthy face was pallid in the red light. There was something of the splendid beast about this fellow, too; a quality that showed even when he faced certain death and no merciful one. He had run, and when overtaken he had fought; and now he must pay.

"Hanglip, to the wheel here!" Dolores commanded. "Six of you bring back the sloop. The rest attend me! Bring the schooner to her course, northwest, Hanglip; and, Spotted Dog, rig me a whip at the foregaff-end. Yellow Rufe, pray or curse while ye may. Thy course is run. There is nothing left to say. Ten minutes remain to thee."

The doomed pirate stood in silence while the preparations were being made; but when Spotted Dog brought down the end of the rope he had rove through the block at the end of the gaff, and stood grinning anticipatively before Dolores, Rufe's tongue came loose, and he burst into a torrent of futile, raving blasphemy.

"Take the rope end forward, and pass it around the bows, so that the rope passes beneath the keel," Dolores ordered, and every eager villain in the band knew now what fate awaited Rufe. The schooner, not being square-rigged, was badly fitted for the operation of keel-hauling; but Dolores's inventive brain had devised a refinement of even that refinement of torture. She waited for the rope end, and when Spotted Dog brought it aft, on the weather side, passing clear from the gaff to leeward, under the keel and up to windward, she stood aside so that the yachtsmen could witness all.

"Tie his hands, Milo!" she said. It was carried out, in spite of Rufe's fierce fight against it. "Now place the noose about his throat tightly." That, too, was done, and now the rope led from Rufe's neck, over the weather rail, under the schooner, and up to the gaff. Three men stood by the hauling part of the rope, and at a gesture from the girl six others joined them. On every face was a little doubt, for none saw exactly what was coming, least of all Rufe.

"Now release him!" said Dolores quietly, and Rufe was left standing alone, his hands tied, but his feet unfettered. He glared around as if he saw a slim chance yet for life; the hope died the next moment, for Dolores signed to the men at the rope, they began hauling, and the terror leaped into Rufe's eyes afresh.

For a moment Venner and his friends saw what they imagined to be a piece of grim jesting; but they, as well as Rufe,speedily saw there was no jest in this. For as the rope tightened, and other roaring ruffians ran joyously to take a pull at it, Rufe was drawn irresistibly toward the weather rail with a choking drag on his throat. He seized the rail, and strained with his every sinew to fight that deadly peril; the rope only tightened more; it was either go or strangle for him; fight as he might, he was forced to climb on the rail, to aid in his own funeral.

The yachtsmen turned dizzy with the awfulness of the man's end; but they could not take their fascinated eyes from the scene. They saw Rufe topple over the rail with a choking curse, and saw the rope pull him under the vessel; they saw the rope quiver to the pirates' lusty pull as the victim was battered against the keel. And they saw the terrible figure leap from the sea to leeward and fly to the gaff-end as the men ran away with the rope to a roaring chorus. But they saw no more. Their eyes refused to look at a repetition of that horror. And Dolores, watching them keenly, came to them, after giving final orders regarding Yellow Rufe's body, took their chains in her hand, and said:

"When again the thought comes to leave me, gentlemen, think well upon what I have showed thee. Now come below. I owe thee some refreshment after a night of storm. 'Twill be approaching dawn ere the schooner can beat back to my haven. Come. I will serve thee with supper."

CHAPTER XV.

THE FIRES OF THE FLESH.

In the schooner's saloon the atmosphere was peaceful by contrast with the hurly-burly outside; yet even here the steep slant of the deck, the shrill, protesting squeal of working frames and beams, the sullen thud and swish of racing seas along the vessel's skin, kept the storm ever in mind: the dizzy plunge of the bows into great gray seas, with its accompanying rise of the stern and the hollow jar and thump of the rudder-post in its port, kept the interior humming with sound as from a distant organ.

Again chained to the mainmast, the three yachtsmen stood gloomily regarding Dolores, whose capable, battle-wise fingers now performed a task more in keeping with her sex and charm. Under the great swing-lamp in the skylight she leaned over the table, mixing wine in low, stout cups, spreading a silver salver with food from the pantry. And a thrilling picture she made in the soft glow of the lamp. The beautiful face was warm with color; the scarlet lips were slightly opened in a brilliant smile; intent upon her task, she swayed with superb grace to the tremendous lurches of the driving schooner, ignoring all outside affairs.

Her preparations completed, she placed tray and cups at the end of the table nearest the mainmast, turned around the deep armchair which had been the owner's own, and sat down, offering a cup and the tray with a little laugh of satisfaction.

"Come, friend Rupert," she said, thrilling Venner again with her vibrant voice, "thou shalt be first. Eat—and drink. See, for thee I do this." She raised the cup to her lips, and kissed the brim, fixing her fathomless eyes full on Venner as she did so.

He struggled with his feelings for a moment, and hated himself heartily for even debating his attitude. But he fell, as he had done before, dazzled by her witchery. His eyes blazed, his blood leaped, and he took the cup with a mumbled attempt at thanks. Dolores smiled at his confusion, and in that smile was the allure of a Circe.

Venner's expression became less tense as he noted the faces of his fellows; for

82

in their eyes he read jealousy, rank and stark, and it warmed him to the marrow. In the next instant his warmth rose to fever heat, and malice twisted his features; Dolores had taken another cup, and now she offered it to Pearse, with a smile yet more gracious than before.

"My silent friend, here's to thee, too," she murmured. His cup she kissed twice, and presented it carefully so that the place she kissed was against his lips. "Drink. I have sweetened it."

As Venner's brows darkened, so did John Pearse conquer his first flush of self-contempt and put on a smile that irradiated his usually serious face. And Tomlin brightened, too, waiting in what patience he could muster for his turn, which must come next. To him Dolores turned, cup in hand, and rising at the same time gave him his wine with a brief: "Here, drink, too. I must leave thee a while."

She forced the cup into Tomlin's trembling fingers, gave him never a glance, but went out of the saloon on her errand.

When he realized she was gone, Craik Tomlin dashed down the wine like a petulant boy, and cursed deeply and fiercely. And not until then did Venner and Pearse awake to the true artistry of the woman; for here, instead of making of Tomlin a raging foe, willing to plot with all the power of his alert brain for their ultimate release, she had aroused a demon of black jealousy in him which promised to set all three by the ears.

Restricted as their movements were, they were forced to nurse whatever feelings Dolores had implanted in them in full sight of each other. And Tomlin left no doubt as to his feelings. At the farthest scope of his chain he flung himself down on the slanting floor and crouched there with dull-glowing eyes bent loweringly upon his friends. Venner laughed awkwardly, and glanced at Pearse; the laugh died away and left a silence between them that was vividly accentuated by the manifold voices of the laboring vessel. For in the swift meeting of eyes, John Pearse and Venner, host and guest, friends to that moment, saw in each other an established rival, a potential foe. Involuntarily they drew apart; and when Dolores returned from the deck she found them spread out like star rays, having nothing in common except a common center.

She gave no sign that she noticed them; but her heavy, fringed lids drooped over eyes brimming with gratification. As she stepped from the stairs the schooner swung upright, the deck overhead thundered to the slamming of booms as she came about, and then the cabin sloped the other way, rolling the scattered wine-cups noisily across the floor. Neither man looked up; but Tomlin's cup rolled so that it struck his foot, and he gave voice to a deep oath, terrible in its uncalled-for savagery. Then

Dolores gave them outward notice for the first time.

With a low, pleasant laugh, she stepped quickly to Tomlin's side, laid a hand on his sullen head, and forced him to look up at her.

"I owe thee something, friend," she smiled, and Tomlin flushed hotly under her close regard. "I treated thee badly in my haste. Come"—she went to the sideboard, filled another cup with wine, and came back, kneeling before Tomlin in the attitude of a slave while her big eyes blazed full into his.

"Drink, for I like thee best," she whispered, sipping the wine and putting the brim, warm from her lips, to his.

And Tomlin drank deeply, greedily, trembling under her close proximity. He felt her hand take his chain, heard the tinkle of links, and knew, without seeing, that she had unlocked his fetters and he was free.

"Now sit here with me, and thou shalt tell me about thy world, my friend, the world thou shalt take me to."

Her soft, thrilling voice set Tomlin's blood leaping; and as she spoke she led him to Venner's great chair and sat him down in it. Then, facing at the length of the table her other two captives, she stood behind the big chair, her arms on the top, leaning low to Tomlin's ear, her lips almost brushing his cheek.

And she whispered to him musically, seductively; her jeweled fingers played with his hair; the soft, warm skin of her arms slid over his neck and face; when, in a frenzy, he reached impulsively for her hand and gripped it, she laughed yet more deliciously and permitted him to hold it.

"Why must you seek another world, Dolores?" Tomlin said hoarsely. "Here you are queen. Out in the greater world you can be no more. Stay, and let me stay with you."

"And would my paltry possessions pay thee for renouncing thy people, thy home?" she asked.

"Home? People? God! I renounce Heaven itself if you say yes!"

"We shall see, my friend," Dolores sighed, and Tomlin felt her tremble slightly. "My chief desire is to leave behind me this life of herder to human beasts. To go into the world whence comes such as thee, Tomlin; to live among the people who can make such as these"—she indicated the rich furnishing of the saloon, the sideboard silver and plate, the stained glass of the skylight.

"All these things I have, and more—nay, but thy treasures are nothing compared with what I shall show thee in the great chamber—yet must I keep them hidden because of the beasts that call me Sultana! Where they came from, these treasures, must be men like thee, Tomlin, women like the painted women of my gallery, people with the art to make these things instead of the brute power to steal them. And there I will go, and thou art to be my guide."

"Then, in Heaven's name, let us go now!" cried Tomlin, trying to rise. She laughed in his ear again, and her soft, warm arms pressed him back in the chair with a power that amazed him. "We shall go, in good season," she whispered. "But—" The rest was murmured so faintly, yet so tremendously audible to his superheated brain, that he drew back and stared up at her with an awful expression of mingled unbelief and horror distorting his face.

"Do you know what you say?" he gasped, and shot an apprehensive glance toward Venner and Pearse.

"Surely, my friend," she crooned. "Thyself alone, of those who came in this ship, may return. If I am desirable, see to it that I can be pleased with thee." Dolores stood up, bent upon him a dazzling smile, leaned as if to kiss his lips, then with a tinkling little ripple of mirth blew a kiss instead and ran up the companion-stairs to the deck.

Tomlin stood glaring after her as if fascinated. His face, deeply flushed a moment before, had gone deathly white; his profile, turned under the lamp toward his companions, showed deeply puckered brows over stony eyes, lips parted as if to utter a cry of horror. And Venner, fuming inwardly, had seen enough to recall some of his badly scattered wits. He called Tomlin by name hoarsely, softly, and exclaimed when he looked around:

"Tomlin, shall we three be ruined body and soul by that sorceress? Come, help us out of these chains, and we will make a bid for liberty. We can reach Peters and such men as are left, by way of the alleyway to the forecastle; I know where weapons are to be got, and we'll put our fate on the cast. Come. Pearse is of a like mind, eh, Pearse?"

Pearse did not reply at once, and Tomlin saved him the trouble; for, recovering himself with a shudder, he put a hand on the companion-rail and started up the stairs with a laugh of contempt.

"I have no concern with your troubles, Venner," he said. "As for liberty, I am free as air. I believe patience is the medicine you need."

Tomlin reached the deck with tingling ears, for even Pearse came out of his reverie to curse him. But curses or benedictions counted nothing at that moment. In every patch of light he saw Dolores's devilishly lovely face; in every swing of the vessel he saw her consummate grace; he was a thirsty man seeking a spring, knowing full well that a draft must kill him. He stood alone outside the companion-way, wondering at the absence of people, at the absence of Dolores. A solitary man stood at the wheel; and, looking around for others, Tomlin noticed vaguely that the black storm was broken, that watery stars were winking down, and that almost in the zenith a gibbous moon leaned like a brimming dipper of quicksilver, ready to drop from the inky cloud that had but just uncovered it.

Then voices reached his ears from forward, voices full of wondering anger, and he stepped out clear of the deck-house and peered ahead on the windward side. There, two miles away, the land loomed black and forbidding; and high up, on a crest, a great red blaze leaped and swirled against the flying clouds.

As he stood, Dolores ran aft, ignoring him utterly in her haste. Her men grouped themselves along the waist of the schooner, waiting for commands. The Feu Follette was already doing her best; that is, the best under such sail as was safe to carry. But there, to windward, and yet two miles distant, some part of the pirate village was burning, and none might say yet what part it was.

The one thing certain was that it could not be the great chamber. That was of rock; it might be destroyed by an explosion; never by fire. So there was a ring of exultation in Dolores's tone when she sent the hail along:

"Loose both topsails and set them! Caliban, thou small villain, out and loose the outer jib. Main-sheet here! Oh, haul, bullies! Flat—more yet—so, belay!"

Then the girl flung the man from the wheel, seized the spokes herself, and began to nurse the schooner to windward with truly superhuman art. Closer yet she brought the graceful craft; closer, until the luffs trembled and the seas burst fair upon the stem and volleyed stinging spray the full length of her. And as she drew nearer, the blaze seemed to diminish and blaze afresh as if fire-fighters were there indeed, but lacking weapons to fight with.

"Is it the treasure-house?" Tomlin asked anxiously, stepping beside the girl. She stood in deep shadow; the dim radiance from the lighted binnacle touched her face, breast, and arms with soft light, and her eyes, as they flashed swiftly toward the man, glittered with some subtle quality that sent a shiver running down his spine.

"Treasure-house?" she repeated, and her voice was no longer soft and alluring; it was metallic and menacing. For the second time, first in Venner, now in Tomlin, she had seen the true source of their fascination. "No, it is not the treasure-house. It is the council hall, where thou wert lodged." She snatched her gaze from the compass and fixed him with the cold, unwinking stare of a snake. "Where thou wert lodged, my friend who would renounce all for me. Where, had I cared to, I might have left two of ye, taking with me to safety only the one whose brains are not afire with soulless gold and jewels."

Tomlin grew hot and uneasy. "My brain is on fire with your beauty, Dolores," he returned, trying to force her gaze to meet his again.

"Prove it to me, then," she replied shortly, and waved him away, devoting her attention now to making the anchorage, already close to.

CHAPTER XVI.

PEARSE ENTERS THE CAVE OF ALADDIN.

Lucky it proved that Pascherette had been left behind when the schooner sailed after Yellow Rufe. Even Dolores, with all her consummate wisdom, had forgotten the existence of the old woman she had degraded to kitchen drudge; still more utterly had she forgotten the relationship existing between the old woman and the late victim of her terrible vengeance.

Sancho had called the old crone mother, whether with blood reasons or not none knew. And at bottom, much of Sancho's rebellion had come of anger at the treatment meted out to her. And it was Sancho's despairing cry, when Milo cast him out into the Grove, that brought the old woman from her concealment in the forest. The awful plight of the unlucky wretch had aroused in the woman's withered breast a demon of revenge that knew no limits; and the departing schooner, then barely visible to her, filled her brain with the knowledge that the strangers who came in that vessel had been the indirect cause of her Sancho's fate.

She knew they had been placed in the cells behind the council hall; she knew nothing of Dolores's last-minute decision that had taken them with her. She knew nothing as to who or how many were left in the camp; but she knew, she had terrible and ever-present proof in that moaning, groping, brainless thing that was Sancho, that her mistress had shown a leaning toward the strangers at the expense of her own people, and that she herself might expect no mercy if ever caught. And with the low animal cunning that served her for intellect she knew her penalty could be no greater if she struck one blow in revenge before taking to the woods in final flight.

Her plan was simple. Watching Sancho for a while, so that she might not lose him, she searched for dry wood among the drenched underbrush, piled it against the rear of the council hall, and set fire to it, fanning the faint flame and feeding it, guarding it with her scanty garments, until the red tongues shot up in a powerful, self-supporting conflagration.

Then she had darted back to the forest fringe, found Sancho, and turned his sightless, blank face toward the blaze so that he might feel the warmth and guess the cause. But she knew nothing of his cracked brain; she knew only of his physical agonies; the utter absence of interest in him when she would have shown him what she had done shook her to the foundations of her own reason; and her eldritch scream pealed up among the trees as she flung her arms aloft and cursed the place.

It was the scream that brought Pascherette out of the hut, where she sheltered from the storm, to see the council hall in flames. It was the scream that told the little octoroon where the fire had birth. And Pascherette, too, believed that the three strangers were still within the cells. She had plans of her own that required the safety of those men, at least for a while. And her active brain gave her the solution before the old woman had ceased to curse.

Like a small, sleek panther Pascherette ran toward the old woman; she saw Sancho, too, but instinctively knew that after Milo's treatment of him he could not be dangerous; ignoring the man, she drew her knife as she ran, and with a brief, panting, "That for thee, witch!" struck the old woman down at Sancho's stumbling feet.

Now she gave all her energies to subduing the fire; and, swiftly rallying every man or woman in the camp she drove them with blows and shrill invective to beating the blaze with sodden boughs and wet sand. She set men with poles to batter down the doors to the cells; but the doors had been built to oppose that kind of entry. Frantically she drove the fire-fighters to another place, while she heaped up fresh fire against the doors in the hope of burning down what could not be burst. And it was the last up-blazing shaft of fire as the doors fell that Dolores saw in the moment she brought the schooner to anchor. Pascherette was emerging, singed and blackened, with dark rage in her glittering eyes at having found the cells empty, when Dolores and her crew arrived on the scene with Venner and Tomlin and Pearse in their midst.

"What! Pascherette again?" cried Dolores, glaring at the girl with red suspicion in her face. "Is this thy work? Speak!"

Pascherette stared in surprise at the three strangers, and her painfully scorched lips strove to answer. Her throat was dry, and at first words refused to come. But in the pause, when fifty faces glowered at the girl, something stumbled across the open in the firelight, and Milo's sharp vision distinguished it. He went up to Pascherette, with deep concern in his devoted eyes, and laid a strong arm about her trembling shoulders. She relaxed toward him, and managed to whisper to him. He flung out his free hand toward the open space, and cried to Dolores:

"There is the traitor, Sultana! This is the avenger."

Dolores looked; every eye was turned where Milo pointed; and the brutal laughter of some of the hardiest pirates mingled with the groans of the three yachtsmen, whose escape from a horrible death by fire could not reconcile them to the staggering vengeance that had overtaken the wretch who had attempted that death. Bathed in an infernal glow, grotesque as a creature of a diseased brain, the unhuman Sancho staggered across the glade and into the darkness of the forest, bearing in his handless arms a ghastly burden in which the hilt of Pascherette's dagger glittered and flashed as the firelight touched it.

"Back! Let him go!" cried Dolores; and a score of shouting ruffians returned from swift pursuit, leaving Sancho and his burden to pass into the oblivion of the great forest.

Milo examined the damage, and reported. The cells were useless now, except merely to confine captives. They did not fit in with Dolores's plans thus, and she sent Milo to a distance with John Pearse while she carried into effect a new fancy.Her crew had gone to their own places, to soothe the fatigues of their night's work in carousal; Pascherette stood near by, gazing at her mistress with mute appeal that she, too, be permitted to seek alleviation of her own sore burns.

"Wait, child," said Dolores, seeing the girl's trouble. "I'll cure thy hurts soon."

Then she separated Venner and Tomlin, taking each in turn to a vacant hut. And to each she whispered patience and faith; to each her voice imparted a renewed thrill. To Venner she said:

"Thy anger with me was foolish, good Rupert. I did but smile at thy friends to make thy task easier. Now see; I leave thee unfettered, and thus." She drew his head down and lightly kissed his hair, laughing with a little tremor: "Think of what I asked of thee, Rupert. To-morrow I shall ask thy decision."

In turn to Tomlin she whispered:

"The night has been arduous for thee. I was impatient with thee. Thy vow of devotion to me rang true, though I doubted it at the moment. To-morrow I will hear what thy heart speaks. To-night, see, I free thee. For thy own safety, though, do not venture beyond these doors save with me. My rascals are fierce creatures of jealousy and suspicion. Good night, friend." Him, too, she left tingling with her kiss, and whatever others in the camp did that night, two men found sleep elusive and vain.

Milo brought Pearse to her at her call, and together they went to the great stone before the chamber. Milo rolled back the rock, while his expression showed uneasiness. But he had learned his lesson when protesting against Pascherette's admission to the cave of mystery, and uttered no warning now.

Pascherette, in spite of her burns, bent a roguish face upon Pearse as that puzzled gentleman waited for some word or motion that should give him the reason for this unexpected favor.

Still Dolores said nothing. The rock rolled away, and Milo stood aside, she entered, touching Pearse on the arm as she passed him, and he followed meekly, Pascherette bringing up the rear with Milo after the giant replaced the great stone. Then Dolores turned back to Pearse, under the soft, red glow of the unseen lamps, and flashed a bewildering smile upon him.

"Wilt believe now that I love thee?" she whispered, and her lids drooped over swimming eyes. "Beyond that great door lies the chamber to enter which costs death. Art afraid?"

"Lead on," replied Pearse hoarsely. There was no trace of fear in his voice or in his eyes; but Dolores warmed gladly to the knowledge that here at last was a man whose thoughts were bent upon her and not on her chamber of treasures.

They stood before the massive sliding door of plate and jewels, and here the human side in John Pearse showed through for an instant. Under the great, yellow lantern the gold and silver plates, the glowing rubies, the glinting emeralds, made a picture of fabulous riches that even he could not ignore. But at the upward slide of the door his eyes left the richness of it without a flicker; he waited for the heavy velvet hangings to be drawn, and when Dolores's eyes sought his they surprised his deep, ardent gaze fastened full on herself and not upon what might next be revealed.

"Enter, man of my heart," she smiled, and stood aside to permit him to pass.

In the first steps over the threshold John Pearse saw little save a dim, cool hall, vast and full of vagrant shadows; then, when Milo had arranged the lights so that they gradually grew in power, flooding the chamber with mellow radiance, his soul seemed to burst from his throat in one choking, stupefied gasp.

"The Cave of Aladdin!" he choked, and stood open-mouthed while Dolores laughed softly at his shoulder.

"Nay," she reproved. "'Tis the Cave of Dolores. 'Tis mine, and"—she turned her face up toward his alluringly—"may be thine, if thou'rt a true man!"

With shrewd artistry she twisted away as he strove to clasp her, and there she left him standing, in the midst of untold treasures that every moment were increasingly revealed to him. Without another glance for him, or apparently another thought, she took Pascherette by the hand and led her down the chamber to the great chair.Here she busied herself with salves and lotions to assuage the scald of the girl's fresh burns, which were more painful than serious. And every moment she was thus charitably employed her gleaming eyes were fixed upon Pearse from under concealing lashes; every moment Milo's dusky face was bent upon her from the end of the chamber with an expression of absolute adoration and gratitude. For tiny Pascherette was custodian of the giant's green heart; and honest Milo never sought very deeply for motives. It was enough for him that Dolores, his Sultana, the being he worshiped as he worshiped his gods, was ministering with woman's infinite tenderness to her maid, a creature as humble as himself.

Pearse, too, even in his intoxication of senses, saw and warmed to this evidence of real womanliness in one he had small cause to think anything other than a be-wilderingly alluring fury. He could not hide his thoughts, and Dolores saw them betrayed on his face; Pascherette surprised the look on her mistress's lovely face that told her the imperious beauty possessed a heart of living flesh and blood. And Pascherette shuddered nervously at the fear of what must happen should that heart ever feel humiliated.

"Keep still, child," Dolores laughed happily, mistaking the reason for the girl's shudder. "It is finished now. Thy hurts will pass in thy sleep. Go to thy big man there, and have him pet thee. I have no need of thee until I call. Go, take him away. I would be alone with my guest."

The girl ran to Milo, and together they went down to the gallery beyond the picture door. Then Dolores set out with her own fair hands wine and sweetmeats, the confections taken from the yacht, strange and new to her, but in her mind some-thing desirable to such men as Pearse, else why had they brought such things? And again using her innate witchery, she set a chair for Pearse at a distance from her own, where she could look straight into his face or hide her own, as her fancy dic-tated.

"Hast seen the like before?" she smiled, looking at him over the brim of a chased gold flagon.

"Never, never, Dolores!" he said, and his eyes blazed into hers. He moved his chair close to her, and reached for her free hand.

"What! Hast thou no eyes for these things?" she exclaimed in simulated sur-prise, taking her hand away and indicating the wealth around the walls. "Man, thy eyes are idle; look at those gems, those paintings; hast ever seen the like of those 'Three Graces,' then, that they have no interest for thee?"

"Yes, I have seen the like, wonderful, wonderful being," he returned hoarsely. "You I have seen; you, you, I see nothing else but you, Dolores!"

She dazzled him with a seductive smile, full of fire-specked softnesses, and of-fered him her flagon.

92

"Drink, comrade. Drink here, and we shall talk of thee and me, and what concerns us both nearly. Art sure thy eyes are not blinded by the nearer beauty?"

"I am not blind! I never saw with clearer vision!" Pearse cried, taking the flagon with tremorless hand. "I care nothing for these tawdry gauds."

"Ah! Then thou'rt the man. Come, thy faithful soul deserves reward. Come, I will show thee treasures thou hast not dreamed of yet; and all shall be thine, with me—at a price."

CHAPTER XVII.

THE TREASURE TEST.

Dolores gaily took John Pearse by the hand and led him down the chamber to the dais on which stood the vacant chair of state of the dead Red Jabez. The great canopied bed still stood there; but it was curtained in, out of sight, and unused; Dolores preferred her own low couch, with its strangely beautiful composite furnishings of silk and tiger-skins, velvet and snowy polar-bear rugs, heaped high with luxurious cushions that made it a restful lounge by day as well as a sleep-inviting couch by night.

Beside the couch, between it and the dais, Milo had set the treasure-chests, leaving the lids wide-flung, the contents butthinly concealed by silken shawls. The end of a rope of matchless pearls hung over the edge of one chest carelessly, without apparent motive; yet when she guided Pearse to the couch and seated him, Dolores scanned his face with glinting eyes that peeped out through narrow slits. She saw his look of interest; then his mouth turned upward in a smile that said plainly: "Here is a theatrical trick to impress me!"

"Now thy reward is come," whispered Dolores, leaving him with an arch smile and kneeling before the big chests. She tore away the shawls and plunged her hands into the glittering hoard to the wrists, flinging out upon the couch and the floor, upon Pearse's knees and into his hands, rubies and emeralds, diamonds and pearls, golden chains and ornaments for the hair in a bewildering, stupendous litter. And, her face turned from him, her narrowed eyes were fixed upon him, and in their gleaming depths burned a smoldering anxiety that was nearing impatience.

For John Pearse cloaked his feelings better than his fellows; he smiled at the shower of riches, met her questing glance with a smile, and smiled again with shaking head when she stood before him, aglow with yearning for his decision, and asked simply:

"Well?"

"Baubles, playthings, Dolores!" he laughed up at her. He seized her hands, stroked the satin-skinned forearm, and said softly: "These are not worthy of such a woman as Dolores. These are but the gauds of a beautiful woman. To fit you, they should be the adornments of a goddess!"

"Oh, then thy lips uttered truth!" she cried delightedly. She stooped swiftly to him, twined her arms about his neck, and laid her warm cheek to his. "Now I shall show thee treasures indeed, my John!"

She ran to the one chest yet unopened, and flung away the silk covering. Here were the gems of the craftsman's art. Stones of unparalleled color and size were in this chest; but their chief merit lay in their cunning settings, their consummate delicacy of workmanship. Here the art collector might find his El Dorado; in all the world such a collection could scarcely be found in one place. Here were shrines and temples, carved from single immense stones or pieces of jade; here was a woven thing of gold and silver, in which the warp and woof lay close as tapestry, portraying as no tapestry could portray it the fabled valley of "Sinbad," in which the sands were gold, the sky silver, and the gems were gems indeed.

"Is this to thy mind?" Dolores cried, tossing to him a golden ball which by some amazing internal mechanism played fairy chimes as it whirled through the air.

Her lips parted in flushed pleasure at the result of her display, for John Pearse was smitten with the collector's fever. He missed her ball through sheer inability to tear his eyes from the other treasures. And as his brain began to grasp the stupendous truth, to more readily estimate values, his eyes turned from the more gaudy works of art, and noticed, for the first time clearly, the pricelessness of many greater things of canvas and wood, ivory and glass, with which the apartment abounded.

"Now thy heart craves my treasures, too, eh?" she chided, gliding to him and laying a hand on his head. Yet she felt glad of his awakened interest. It was merely another card she might yet have to play.

"Astounding!" he gasped. His gaze fastened upon a boule bric-à-brac stand, on which stood an Aretine vase two feet high, of peerless form and glaze. The ticking of the great Peter Hele clock drew his attention to a work of ebony and ivory as scarcely could be believed as coming from man's hands.

"Now thou'rt of a kind with thy fellows!" she cried in anger. "Look at me! No, thy eyes will not deign to seek me now!"

Pearse snatched his eyes away, and answered her with a laugh that sent her blood leaping again.

"My Dolores forgets she demanded my admiration for her treasures," he said. "What would you have, splendid one? Shall I say these treasures are still paltry, when I see their countless worth? Still I say you are the treasure beyond price. These are but a little more fitting for you. That is all. Am I forgiven?"

He leaped to his feet, seized her hand, and attempted to slip an arm about her waist. She, lithe as a leopard, slipped from his grasp with a glad laugh that rippled in a low murmur to his hot ears, and intensified the glare that had come into his eyes. She failed to see that glare. It was the glare of greed; stark and utter greed, that counted no cost and brooked no opposition in driving for its ends.

"Thou art forgiven indeed!" she replied, panting and disheveled, a thing of wondrous loveliness. "So far art thou forgiven that I shall put thy heart to the grand test at once. Of thy fellows none can compare with thee for scorn of wealth and desire of me. Sit down again, my man; let us reveal our inmost hearts to each other."

She told him, keeping him at provoking distance, of her heart-hunger for the outside world, the world of art and things of beauty. She thrilled him with her vibrant voice, mesmerized him with her distant, caressing touch and glorious, limpid eyes. She made his blood pulse hotly with desire with her soft-spoken offer of self-surrender to the man who should lead her from her sovereignty over human beasts and set her feet in the high places of the earth.

"And with these my treasures, I shall make my man a king in truth," she said, slipping along the couch toward him and laying both hands clasped on his arm. She threw back her head, shaking loose her great masses of lustrous hair, and poured her soul at him from half-closed, moist eyes that gleamed like midnight pools in starlight. "Yet must my chosen man assure me of his love for me, and his contempt for my riches. For, though my treasures shall be his, yet will I be first in his heart or forget him."

"And first you are, and shall be, Dolores," whispered Pearse, leaning his chin on her forehead and glaring covetously at the littered wealth of the chests. "What man of warm blood can see any other being or thing when Dolores is by?"

"Then come. I believe thee," she said, rising slowly. "Come with me, my man above price. See here."

She swept back a piece of tapestry at the rear of the chamber, and disclosed a dark and gloomy cavern, hewn out of the solid rock, as was the greater cavern. From a brazier she took a pine splinter, lighted it, and beckoned Pearse into the cave. And as soon as his eyes adjusted themselves to the gloom, he saw the place stowed tightly from floor to ceiling with kegs and half-casks, hooped and marked with black characters.

"Gold?" he gasped, perspiration starting to his brows.

"Gold!" Her rejoinder was tense, almost savage; she glared at him from under the torch, a quivering shape of disgust.

96

"Why, Dolores, don't look like that," he laughed. "I did but wonder. If this were all gold, it could not enhance your worth in my eyes."

"Then the proof will be easy. This is not gold. It is gunpowder. Our whole store. My rascals are not to be trusted with more powder than they can use at once. From this store I dole them out their rounds; thus are all safe. But at this moment I have other use for this powder. Stay here; or no, help me. It will be finished the sooner."

Dolores ran out into the great chamber again, Pearse following her wonderingly. She left him in wonder but a short time; for, gathering up a great armful of treasure she started back to the cave, crying: "Come, fill thy arms, too." He paused, and she took up his hesitation swiftly, feeling again a surge of doubt and disgust rise in her breast. She called to him, scornfully: "What, art afraid? Come, faint one; beyond here is my secret outlet from this place. Now art satisfied?"

And John Pearse followed into the cave, a-tingle with the hope that he was indeed the elect. He saw her fling her riches down on the tops of the kegs; she bade him do likewise, and then led the way back for more. And so she went, and so he followed; journey after journey was completed, until the gunpowder-kegs were almost buried beneath the wealth of an empire. Then the girl stepped outside, and called Milo. The giant appeared with silent speed.

"Milo, burst me one of these kegs," sheordered, and her voice forced Pearse's attention; it was so cold, passionless, utterly controlled. The keg was burst, and a trickle of coarse cannon powder ran on the floor.

"Lay a damp train out to the ledge over the grove, Milo!"

Milo disappeared through the gallery, trickling moistened powder from his fingers as he went. Then, when his voice sounded back along the passage, Dolores again took Pearse by the arm and said, looking him full in the eyes: "Thy test, friend. Here am I. Out there is the grove, and beyond it the sea. Take this torch. Put light to the powder train, and thou and I will depart in the white schooner. We shall leave nothing for these vultures to fight over. But together we will go far away into thy world, thee and me."

"And leave my friends here?" he asked, huskily.

"Ay, my man, but not alive!" she whispered, thrusting her dark, flushed face close to his, and letting her lips breathe their fragrance upon him. "They, thy friends, are not as my beasts. They have the brains of the white kings of the earth; they have the cunning which makes of all other races slaves and dependents. Leave them here, living, and in a day they will rule these rabble and together they will hunt us down. Come, haste. Put thy fire to the train."

"Not yet! Tell me what deviltry is to be worked upon my companions."

"Hah! Then thou'rt but lukewarm in thy love. Am I not Dolores? Am I not worth thy two friends? Listen, I'll tell thee my price, friend. If thy friends are to live, then destroy this trash ere we go, so that they get it not. If thy heart is bent upon saving this treasure, then thy hand must first put thy friends into their long sleep. Nay, peace! There is no alternative. The man who mates with me shall be a man indeed; no petty, squeamish lover whose weak heart sickens at removing a rival."

"Give me until morning," he replied, dry of throat, and pallid of face. "It is a terrible thing you ask, Dolores. Yet I dare not say the cost is too high. As for destroying these treasures, that I know is but a trick to try me. You could never go out into a new world and take a low station. That you would have to do if I set fire to that train." He suddenly darted a look of fierce challenge at her, "There!" he cried. "The trial is yours!"

He flung down his torch, and the powder-train began to splutter and fizz. Dolores flashed a look of approval at him, and burst into a ringing, happy laugh. She kicked aside the torch, and trampled out and relaid the train; then ran to Pearse impulsively, and said with simple earnestness that utterly deceived him:

"Now I believe in thee again, and for ever. 'Twas but to try thee, John. We will leave nothing of worth when we go. But that makes it the more imperative that thy friends have no power to harm us afterward. Think not that Dolores will take a lower station. I shall be queen wherever I go, and my man shall be made a king by my power.

"I give thee until noon to think over thy answer. Go, and the gods protect thee and make thee faithful to me."

Calling Milo back, she bade him conduct Pearse from the great chamber, and as they passed out, little Pascherette peered up at Pearse with an impudent smile, and with her head on one side like a bird she chattered:

"White stranger, thou'rt a fool! What Dolores wills, will surely come to pass. If thy heart fails thee, and thy friends are safe at thy hands, dost think they will have like scruples? Fool again! One of them will kill thee and the other, and that man will gain a peerless mate. And, bend down thy tall head, thou imitation giant—already thy two friends are liberated, each seeking the life of the other, though neither knows of the other's freedom!"

"What?" stammered Pearse, gripping the girl's slim shoulder fiercely. "If you lie—"

"Pshaw! One need not lie to befool thee!" Pascherette retorted scornfully. "Sleep, and if thy throat is not yet slit on thy awakening, make thy decision quickly, and tell it to Dolores."

Pearse would have answered her with more questioning, but she laughed at him, and bade Milo shut him out. So the greatrock fell, and Pearse wandered into the camp, not knowing where he went, and caring little. He had no place to sleep, so far as he knew; yet he felt no wonder. He walked through the sleeping-camp, across the grove, and into the forest, his brain on fire and seething with the problem before him.

"The treasure, with or without the woman!" he muttered, clenching his hands savagely. "The treasure! Ye gods! There must be the wealth of Monte Cristo there!" He broke off into a harsh laugh at thought of his challenge with the torch. "The witch!" he chuckled. "She was clever, but John Pearse overreached her. Now I know her heart. But—"

He wandered on, and his mind was centered upon Venner and Tomlin. The more he thought over the situation, the more he found his ideas forming themselves after Dolores's.

"Why should I share it?" he asked of the winking stars.

And while he communed with himself regarding her and her demands, Dolores overlooked Milo in a task that brought a sparkle to her eyes and a gleaming smile to her lips. They were repacking the great treasure chests.

CHAPTER XVIII.

PASCHERETTE DEALS AGAIN.

Dolores spent her night in slumber as peaceful as a babe's. When Milo had completed his task with the treasure chests he went to his own couch. John Pearse wandered deep into the eery forest, his brain filled with tumultuous fancies, while Craik Tomlin and Rupert Venner lay in the dark before the open doors of their separate cells, struggling for a decision with their own good and evil natures. But Dolores, before retiring called Pascherette to dress her hair and gave the little octoroon some secret instructions against the morning.

"Now to thy bed, girl, and wake with bright eyes," said Dolores, her toilet completed. "Let thy busy tongue wag its liveliest then; see to it that the strangers hear whispers and rumors, yet keep them apart and from harm a while. Thy task with the other rabble is easy. I care not how they are divided. But divided they must be; to the point of mutiny. Go, and sweet dreams to thee."

It was then that a subtle happiness stole into Dolores's face; then her great luminous eyes closed slowly in utter peace; then that she lay down with a gentle sigh on her couch of furs and slept care-free and smiling.

Dreams not of the brightest might have ruffled her calm had she seen the night watch of her maid. For the moment Pascherette was dismissed, and gave a second thought to her orders, a light of dawning hope, prospective triumph, broke over the small, gold-tinted face and sleepiness fled for the night.

"Divided they shall be!" she whispered, and hugged herself rapturously. "Divided to her disaster and—Milo's triumph!"

Then the maid wrapped herself in a robe, and went out to the camp.

Like a fantom she appeared to Venner, and as swiftly vanished; but in the moment that she bent over him she whispered in his ear that Tomlin was the chosen of Dolores; that he and Pearse were doomed at the hands of their friend.

"I tell thee, watch," she said. "By noon to-morrow the truth shall be shown to thee." And in leaving him she placed in his hands the rapier that had been taken

100

from him by Dolores.

To Tomlin next she appeared, and his rapier also she returned; but in his ear was breathed the name of John Pearse. To find Pearse himself was harder; but she waited, and shortly before the dawn he emerged from the forest and walked dully toward his own charred cell.

"Hah, my friend," she said to him, suddenly appearing from the shades. "I fear thy tardiness has defeated thee. Now thou'lt need to look to thyself, for the man Venner has vowed thy life to Dolores, and that of Tomlin."

"What! Venner?"

"Surely. Why not? Is not Dolores worthy such a sacrifice then? Hah, but Venner is a man of decision. Thy eyes sawthe treasure? It's lost to thee—unless—" she whispered, peering up into his angry face.

"Unless?"

"Unless thou prove the better man. Dolores would have thee before all the rest, friend; but she despises a waverer. I tell thee thy fortune is yet in thy hands."

"How?"

"Here, I have thy sword. Take it, and keep aloof and watch. When thou canst see men carrying the treasure chests out to the white vessel, then will be the time to strike. Join thyself with the men who seem faithful to my mistress. There will be fighting; and the spoils are for the victor."

Pearse would have stayed her, but she ran from him with a tantalizing laugh and vanished into the women's quarters.

In the morning, when the men had breakfasted, a hum of activity pervaded the place which was attributable to the octoroon's subtle influence. As if by prearrangement, men drew apart into little knots, each gathering about a leader and showing indecision until each man ascertained exactly where his fellows were going. Then Dolores appeared with Milo, and she faced four distinct parties before the great stone.

The sun was metallic in its redness, rising from behind a group of low-hanging, hazy clouds, casting its fierce beams on the point and the low shores of the anchorage. A brazen sky overtopped the scene, giving to green foliage and yellow sands alike, a glare as of terrific artificial light.

As Dolores appeared, the party headed by Caliban stepped forward, muttering angrily, and every man kept hand on knife or cutlass. Caliban himself, nervous and yet determined, glared at the formidable giant and suddenly sprang out alone, shaking his first at Milo, and working himself into greater fury. A frown darkened the face of Dolores; she had commanded Pascherette to bring about a condition of unrest, but nothing like this; for in all four parties was an attitude of suspicion of herself, not of each other. She spoke in a low voice to Milo, then raised her hand and advanced toward Caliban.

"Well, whelp of a deformed dog!" she cried. "What do ye seek with me? Is this the way I've taught thee to beg?"

"I beg nothing!" screamed Caliban, pacing to and fro restlessly. "We demand, not beg!"

"Demand? Have a care for thy loose tongue!"

"My tongue's my own! We are tired of thy trumpery state. Tired of thy mystery and falsity. We know thy plot—know thy cunning scheme to carry thy favorites away from here—to carry away the treasure that is ours, not thine! Think ye we men will let ye go, to set the dogs of war-ships upon us? Here and now we demand a settlement."

"Demand, again? Good Caliban"—she said softly, and smiled upon him—"thy training has been faulty. Come, I will answer thee."

"Ye answer us all, or none. I know thee too well to trust thee. Answer these men, who ask thy reason for keeping these three strangers to the detriment of thine own people. Sancho paid dearly for his sight of thy great chamber. Did the stranger who was in there with thee last night suffer, too?"

"That's the talk; answer!" shouted the crew, led by Caliban's band and supported less vociferously by the rest.

"Silence, then; I will answer!" cried Dolores, quivering with suppressed rage. She spoke again to Milo, then turned to face the mob, her head erect, her eyes ablaze.

She flashed a keen glance toward Pearse, who had sidled over to the band led by Stumpy, who seemed less accusative than the others; she nodded faintly, approvingly, and sought the others. Venner stood aloof, on the fringe of Hanglip's crowd; Tomlin stood almost by the side of Spotted Dog.

"I will answer. I see among ye men of troubled minds, who are not yet disposed to flout my authority. Thee, Caliban, I have forgiven before; yet here thou art, venturing again to confront me with demands. I will not reply to thee, nor to any one man or party. To ye all, my people, I have my answer. In one hour, in the grove, ye shall hear and be satisfied. That is my answer now. Come Milo."

She walked slowly and steadily straight through the midst of the muttering, grumbling mob, Milo at her back like a gargantuan shadow. And looking neither to one way or the other, meeting eyes that glared in her path with cold, dignified disdain, she proceeded through the camp, across the grove, and to the ledge behind the altar. Savage curses followed her; men jostled at her heels and dared Milo to prevent them; the giant, calm and cold as his mistress, moved forward like a human Juggernaut, laying a resistless hand upon a presuming shoulder here, flinging aside a leering ruffian there.

And as the mob thinned, and Dolores entered the cool glade, something in the situation which she had failed to realize before now struck her with force; she started at the thought, then uttered a low, rippling laugh of satisfaction. For Pascherette, in her cunning scheme of double-dealing, had played into her lady's hands to an extent unhoped for by Dolores.

"Milo, the wolves are ready to tear," she said. "And they shall tear—not me, but themselves! Didst note the three strangers? Even they shall help more than I had hoped." She stepped up behind the altar, and as she waited for Milo's assistance in climbing to the secret entrance to the great chamber she asked:

"Thy blow-pipe, hast forgotten its use."

"As soon forget the use of my fingers, Sultana!" replied the giant, permitting a grim smile to wrinkle his face for an instant.

"Then get thy darts. Have thy pipe ready here, thyself concealed, and watch thy time to strike. But first light the altar fires. The rogues believe in my magic no longer; I shall teach them anew, and such magic as shall convince some of them."

From the camp arose a babel of uproar, men shouting against each other, curses and threats alike aimed broadcast. And impatient of the delay, small groups straggled into the grove to wait, Stumpy's party first, their leader striving fiercely to quiet their noise. Dolores reappeared soon, dressed in her altar robe, and her flashing eyes told her quickly that John Pearse wavered between staying with his chosen party and going in search of his companions. She caught his eye, and smiled brightly at him, beckoning him to her.

He went up to the altar slowly, his face dark and sullen. She waited for him, ignoring the mutterings of the pirates, and as he approached her she gave him her hand.

"My friend, it pleases me to see thee among my faithful ones. Hast made thy decision?"

"Decision! False woman, the decision was made while yet I was with you. The decision was yours, not mine."

"False? Why, good John, what does that mean?" she asked, frank surprise on her face.

"Have you not taken Venner for your man? Is he not your chosen mate, at the price of my life and Tomlin's?"

"Fool!" she cried, fiercely. "Thy dreams have mixed thy brains. What nonsense is this? I told thee thou wert my man, at a price. But thy decision! Time is short. Say quickly what thou wilt do."

"Prove to me that I have heard that which is untrue, and I give you my answer at the hour you demanded it—at noon."

"If thou remain here, the proof shall be shown thee," she replied, dark with passion. Not yet had she quite seen through the cunning of Pascherette. And a growing tumult beyond the trees warned her of greater stress at hand, she had no more time to spare in argument with Pearse. She waved him back, and with fire in her eyes commanded Stumpy to take his men to one side.

"Stand there! Thy rascals will not dare to flout me!"

"We don't want to, lady," growled Stumpy, sullenly. He motioned his men to follow, and took up a position at the right of the altar. But he glared fearlessly at Dolores as he went, and added: "Ye have none more faithful than Stumpy, if thy heart is still with us and for us. But things begin to look plaguey rough, Dolores, since ye spared the white schooner and her owner."

Swiftly Dolores stepped down and glided to Stumpy's side, his men drawing back involuntarily, not in sufficient numbers to be able to cast off their old awe of her.

"Thy ear, good Stumpy," she whispered. "Art for thy fellow pirates, or for me? Speak quickly."

"I'm for you, lady," he replied, shifting awkwardly on his mutilated foot. "For you, but not if what we heard is true."

"I tell thee it was false. Now art for me?" She bent upon him a smile of dazzling beauty, soft-eyed and almost tender, and the pirate's face grew ashamed; he knelt at her feet in humble obeisance, and the girl laid her hand on his head, and bade him rise.

"Then remain faithful, Stumpy, and thou and thy men shall share in my fortunes. Look well to the stranger there. Keep him with thee. I hear the vultures coming."

She returned to the altar, took her place behind the swirling smoke, and stood motionless, awaiting the arrival of the crowd whose noisy progress could be traced step by step. And presently they broke into the grove, unawed and uproarious, Caliban leading. Still the parties kept apart. Hanglip and Spotted Dog ranged themselves on either side of Caliban's gang, and every eye glared redly at the statuesque figure at the altar.

"Answer! Give us yer answer!" cried Caliban.

"Hear, my people!" Dolores cried, raising her arms for silence. "My answer is this. Among ye is a traitor. That traitor has spread lies among ye. Ye are my people, and none other. Did I not save the white ship for ye? What if I preserved her people. They are here, and here they shall remain. Had I thought to desert ye, could I not have gone in the night? Who should say no? Am I not queen of ye all? Then why this childish talk of leaving ye?"

Dolores was carefully fighting for time; she wished to dissect the feeling of the crowd before her, and while she spoke her irrelevant nothings, her keen eyes roved over every face. And Spotted Dog drew and held her gaze as no other did; his face was awork with savage unbelief, his loose lips wreathed and curled in his impatience to speak. At last his fury could not be longer restrained; he sprang to the front, and howled:

"Lies, all lies! Thy chit of a maid—"

The words were choked in his throat with terrible suddenness. Like something unearthly, reaching from the unknown, the hand of death gripped Spotted Dog and he stumbled and fell forward, gnashing his teeth and clawing futilely at his breast. Dolores did not move. Her expression did not change. Milo had again proved faithful.

But others of Spotted Dog's band, the greatest malcontents, stood forward and peered down at their fallen leader; then with a shout of rage they leaped up, faced the altar, and urged their fellows on.

"More infernal witchcraft!" they cried. "Tear the black witch and her altar down!"

A moment of frightful silence followed, for the speakers felt the same mysterious hand that had reached for and grasped their leader. One by one they dropped in their tracks, smitten none knew how or whence; and even Pearse, with Stumpy's band, shivered at the terrible uncanniness of it. Then Caliban shook off his terror, sensed human agency in the silent death, and looked around for the hand that sped it. As he glared, a dart entered his own breast; but this one, ill-sped, failed in its mission. The pirate staggered, his eyes widened, then he seized the protruding dart. For an instant he hesitated; then taking the direction indicated by the slanting missile, he flung an arm toward Stumpy's crew and howled:

"There's the dog! There's the sudden death! Tear 'em up, bullies! Pull Stumpy down!"

In an instant the grove seethed with a terrific conflict, in which Stumpy's party was set upon by three times the number. And John Pearse was carried into the thick of the fight; unwilling or not, his skilled rapier began to take toll of the roaring furies about him. And while the battle raged, and Dolores stood calmly looking on, one of the pirates whose duties had kept him at the anchorage of the schooner appeared with a rush upon the scene and shouted:

"Lads, ye're being fooled! The slaves are even now taking the treasure down to the schooner!"

CHAPTER XIX.

WHILE VICTORY HANGS IN THE BALANCE.

The cry rang through the Grove like a trumpet call, and the fight was stayed instantly. Every eye flashed upon the bringer of the news, and behind him stood Pascherette, partly hidden by the trees, her small, eager face peering from behind a trunk. And as she took in the scene, a great terror stole into her eyes and her lips opened in a gasp.

The octoroon had played her great coup. She had carried a lie to the pirate, hoping that his telling of the treasure to his fellows would precipitate such an assault upon Dolores that nothing could survive it. Now she saw the attack already launched without her connivance; she saw the pirate, dead, and saw Stumpy and one of the strangers stoutly defending the queen.

As she stared, at a loss, Caliban staggered out in front again, clutching at his wound, and screamed:

"Satan seize ye if that witch escapes ye now! Tear her down! Tear her down! Then none can keep the treasure from ye."

His last word ended in a sob. From the hidden giant another dart was sped truer, and Caliban pitched headlong on the steps of the altar. And Pascherette, terrified now that they would leave their work incomplete, swarm after the false treasure report, and thus leave her at the mercy of the enraged Dolores, frantically sought for Milo among the press. She knew nothing of his secret duty with the blow-pipe: seeing nothing of him among the defenders, she surmised he was inside on other duty bent. In desperation she placed all upon a single hazard, and, running out into the Grove she screamed:

"The man lies! It is a lie, to make ye forego thy vengeance. There is no treasure taken away. Make thy work complete!"

A medley of conflicting cries arose as the pirates again separated into three parties. Hanglip's crew, with those of the fallen Caliban, detached themselves from the rest and from two sides threatened the altar, where Dolores stood like a statue, glaring at her maid with deadly fury. Hanglip himself seemed irresolute in the face of the maid's denial; he stood with cutlas raised, not yet sure whether to attack or first see to the treasure story. The decision was made for him; for the pirate bringing the news, seized Pascherette in a fierce grip, and with knife at her breast shouted:

"This little snake told me the loot was going, lads! Get the job over, as I do this!"

Pascherette squirmed in the pirate's grasp, but all her cunning now could not avail her. The knife flashed downward, and she fell to her knees, her tiny golden hands pressed to her side, blood trickling through her fingers. And her face froze in a mask of horror when from behind Dolores stepped Milo, armed with a great broad-ax, and bent his deep black eyes full upon her with terrible accusation in them.

The giant saw the coming storm, and knew the futility of trying to stem it with his blow-pipe. He emerged, armed with his ax, at the moment when the pirates, answering their mate's cry with a shout, surged up the altar steps with blood in their eyes.

Dolores now shook off her seeming unconcern, and with alert vision took in the tremendous crisis. Stumpy's band, with Pearse at their leader's side, had been driven back in the first attack to the rock itself; and now stood with their backs to it grimly waiting for the second onset. They had fought hitherto for her; she saw to it that they did not change their allegiance. Leaping up to the ledge behind the altar, she cried:

"Stumpy! Thou'rt my man. Bring thy fellows up here; one man may hold a score here. Milo! Make way for my faithful ones!"

With Stumpy on the ledge, and his score of men, the battle became dead for the moment. Few of the pirates had firearms, except on forays, and then their ammunition was doled out to them. By this means they had ever been kept in subjection; and now the plan was to prove their undoing;for they could not reach their prey, whose cutlas points presented an insurmountable barrier to their storming the rock. And with John Pearse up there among the defenders, Tomlin and Venner found themselves wondering just what their own position was. They, unblinded by the rage of the pirates, saw the futility of storming that rocky wall with steel, and in the momentary hush and indecision they withdrew from the mob and stood apart, thinking over what was to come.

To Dolores, the hesitation of her foes was something she could not brook, for her great hope now was to set her rascals at each other's throats to their ultimate annihilation. She whispered into Milo's ear.

"Get thy blow-pipe again. Send a dart into Hanglip's black throat, and let every man see how 'tis done."

The giant obeyed. The slender, six-inch dart sped fair to its mark, and Hanglip dropped. But as he fell his eyes saw, as did his men, whence had come the mysterious death that had already taken heavy toll among them. And Dolores saw her plan work to amazing effect; for Hanglip, with his last wheezing breath, raised himself on his elbow, and barked:

"Now ye see the magic! 'Tis but a man's breath. Up, lads, and take pay for me!"

The assault started in grim, silent fury. In waves the attackers mounted the altar; men gave comrades backs, flung them upward, only to catch them again as they recoiled from the steel of the defense like broken seas at a rock base.

But as the fight advanced, and stricken men were piled high on the great altar, attacking steel reached higher and began to reap results. Stumpy's men, now fully persuaded of their queen's regard for them, fought like paladins, roaring out their rough sea-cries as they cut and stabbed with increasing gusto. Even Pearse fell under the spell of fierce action; his rapier played among the heavier strokes of cutlas and broad-knife like summer lightning. And did a hardy pirate gain the ledge in spite of all, there stood Milo, like a bronze Fate, with deadly ax poised to turn success into death. Yet Stumpy's little band grew less; and Dolores, standing over all like an Angel of Doom, saw that something must be done speedily unless she was to be left with too great a number of survivors from this lucky conflict.

"Make a swift assault, Stumpy. Milo, swing that great ax of thine for only five minutes," she said. Then when the fight raged higher yet, she drew Pearse by the arm into the secret entrance.

"Here, friend, are muskets and pistols. Load them while I pass them out. We shall see how hungry for our blood these wolves are."

She showed him the store of arms, in a small cave next to the powder store, and musket powder and bullets were also there. As he loaded the weapons, she passed them out in armfuls, then gave Stumpy a flask of powder for priming, and told him to hold out until Milo could bring up other resources as yet unknown.

"And," she said, leading Stumpy inside for a moment, "here you see a powder-train. There, on the floor. Now hear me, my faithful one, should thy foes still beat thee back, bring all thy men along this passage, but before ye come, touch a fire to this train. I shall await thee at the end, Stumpy, and together we shall see these dogs destroyed."

She called Milo, gave him a command, and then took Pearse with her into the great chamber. Here she answered his questioning glance with a soft smile, and seated him in the great chair.

"Thy sword has done nobly, good John," she said, laying her hand on his head. "The peril is over now. Rest. In a little while Milo will have that which will fill these hungry dogs to the gullet. Rest here. I'll soon be with thee." She leaned down, laid her lips lightly on his face, and whispered: "And be of good cheer; the end is in sight for thee and me."

She left him sitting there, wrapped in his confused thoughts. Then she flew to help Milo with his new engine of war which was to decide the day. From a corner of the apartment the giant dragged a brass culverin, mounted on a swivel, stolen from the poop-rail of some tall Indiaman in years gone by. This was charged with powder, and Milo searched for effective missiles for it. He brought a handful of musket balls to Dolores; she shook her head decidedly after a moment's thought and objected: "Those round pellets are too merciful for such cattle. What do they want? Treasure! Give them treasure, good Milo—their fill of it." As she spoke she ran swiftly into the treasure chamber and seized handfuls of gold chains, while at her command Milo followed her with great gold coins in his huge hands. These they rammed into the cannon, until links of gold fell from the muzzle; then Dolores regarded the terrible thing with a mirthless laugh and bade Milo get to work with it.

"Bid thy men fall back into the gallery as if beaten," she said. "And when the vile bodies of those howling wolves fill the opening, deliver the treasure to them, and may their souls be shattered with their bodies! And that none may remain to repeat this day's mischief, when they break and fly loose, Stumpy and his dogs shall harry them and pursue them into the depths of the forest. Let the maroons finish what we so well begin. See thy gun does not harm the— Wait," she cried, "hold thy artillery until ye see me across the Grove! I shall give thee a sign, then loose thy hell-blast."

Leaving Milo, she ran again through the great chamber and out by the rock door, which was rolled aside and standing open. Then around the mass of the mountain and skirting the grove, past the prostrate Pascherette she sped, casting a glance of bitter hate at the sorely wounded octoroon, but never halting until she reached a point of the underbrush immediately behind the spot where Venner and Tomlin still ranged back and forth uneasily watching the fight.

She rustled the foliage noisily, and the two men swung around in alarm. She thrust her head through the leafy screen, and showed them her face full of tender solicitude. Her great dark eyes were very soft; her scarlet lips were parted in a rosy smile. Venner glared at her, then flashed a glance of reawakening distrust at Tomlin, who returned it tenfold.

110

"Peace, good friends," she said, softly, laying a finger on her lips and nodding toward the raging battle. "Come with me. Both of ye. The day goes badly with me, and I would undo much that I have done toward ye. Come quickly, and with caution."

A momentary distrust for her made them hesitate; then she whispered intensely: "Haste. This is your opportunity."

Venner first shook off his moodiness and followed her into the brush; and Tomlin was close behind him. When she had them in covert, she stepped out once more, waited to catch Milo's eye at the ledge, then gave him the sign. And the defenders fell back as if suddenly broken and beaten. She waited still, until the attackers swarmed over their own dead, stamping over her altar, and gained the entrance, where they crowded in a milling, roaring mass. Then she glided back to the underbrush and said tersely:

"Come!"

Venner and Tomlin walked on either side of her, not caring to meet each other's eye, for their subjection to Dolores's spell was complete whenever in close proximity to her. Hurriedly she led them around the cliff to the great entrance, beyond which they had never stepped. And they went full of tremendous hopes and suspicions, in which the hope predominated; they failed even to cast a look at their schooner, then lying free at anchor, with a few men visible on her decks. Three of the pirates' long boats lay on the shore abreast of her.

They stood in the entrance to the great chamber, sensing some of the awe that filled the mysterious place, peering into the gloom where the ruby lights now failed to cast their glow in the broader light of day entering the open aperture. Dolores led them in with a gesture and a smile, and they reached the massive plated sliding door and stood beneath the yellow lantern, gazing in speechless wonder at the richness of that barrier. And while they waited, mystified and uneasy, from beyond the mountain came the crash of Milo's gun, and the tremendous discharge reverberated through and through the rock, making the passage where they stood rumble and quake as if the mountain were about to fall.

Their faces went white, and Dolores gavethem a reassuring clasp of the hand while she pressed the side-post of the door and started the pulley and weight mechanism that would give them entry.

"Welcome, friends. Enter," she smiled, standing aside to permit them to pass. And Rupert Vernier and Craik Tomlin, forgetting their gloomy thoughts regarding each other, entered the great chamber, and were brought to a sudden halt at the sight of John Pearse sitting at his ease through the strife in the high chair of state.

111

CHAPTER XX.

DOLORES DEMANDS A DECISION.

Milo let loose his infernal blast, and the smashing report was followed by a hush as of death. Then through the blinding and choking powder-reek came the groans and shrieks of the mutilated wretches whose evil fate had placed them in the path of the horribly despatched treasure. The eye could not penetrate the smoke that filled the narrow rock passage; Stumpy and his men were blackened and smeared with smoke and sweat, demoniacal to the ultimate degree; and these were the men Milo hurled forth now to make the *débâcle* complete.

"Out upon them!" he cried, urging Stumpy to the ledge. "Leave not one of these dogs alive, Stumpy, and thy fortune is made. Thy Sultana will reward thee magnificently. Out with ye!"

Stumpy hitched his poor clubfoot along in brave haste, and flourished his cutlas in a hand that dripped red. For once in his stormy life the crippled pirate felt something of the glow that pervaded the heart of devoted Milo: for a moment he felt he was redeeming himself by enlisting his undoubted courage in a worthy cause.

"At 'em, lads!" he roared, leaping down through the smoke. "Dolores, Dolores! Give 'em hell, bullies!"

He stumbled and fell, his crippled foot playing him false. He sprang up with a curse of pain, bit hard on his lip, and plunged into the huddled remnants of the attackers, his roaring bullies at his heels. His onslaught was the one thing needed to put terror into the hearts of the survivors of Milo's blast. Coming through the leek like so many devils, Stumpy and his crew put their foes to flight and followed eagerly, hungrily; the forest rang and echoed with the clash of action and the smashing of underbrush in panicky flight.

Now Milo, his duty to his Sultana performed, thought of Pascherette. The little octoroon lay where she had fallen, a pitiful little huddled heap; never once had her pain-dulled eyes left the giant, or the place where he might appear. And now she saw him coming toward her, not as a ministering angel, but like a figure of wrath, swinging his great broad-ax in one hand as easily as another man might swing a cutlas. She shivered as he stood over her, accusing.

"Milo!" she panted, gazing up at his magnificent height in plaintive supplication.

"Serpent!" he replied, and the utter contempt in his voice went to her heart like a sword-thrust. "Hast a God to pray to before I send thy false soul adrift?"

"I have but one God, Milo; to Him I should not pray."

She fixed her burning gaze upon him, and in her pained eyes blazed all the tremendous love that actuated her small being.

"A God thou canst not pray to, traitor? Art afraid, then?"

"Not afraid, Milo," she whispered, and her eyelids drooped. "I cannot pray to one who looks down upon me as thou dost."

"I?" The giant's expression changed to frowning displeasure rather than anger. "I?" he repeated.

"Thee, my heart. Thou'rt my god, my all. For thee I have done this thing. For thee, who even now canst not see where lies the falsity. Milo"—her weak voice sank to a low murmur—"I beg thy forgiveness. My love for thee caused me to sin. My life is to pay the supreme price. Let me die at least in thy forgiveness."

"Forgive? Forgive thee, who worked for the destruction of the being I worship? Rather shall I speed thy soul!"

Pascherette struggled to a kneeling position, crossed her tiny hands on her panting breast, and looked full into his eyes as a wounded hart looks at the hunter. Her lip quivered, her small, gold-tinted face, once so piquant and full of allure, had taken on a gray hue from her pain, but there was no hiding the great, overwhelming love for the giant that gleamed in her eyes.

"Milo," she said, and the word was a caress, "Milo, if thou must, strike swiftly. Yet again I ask, forgive."

The giant slowly lowered his great ax, and his honest heart answered the pitiful plea. His deep chest swelled and throbbed; into his face crept the look that had been there on that day when he told Pascherette he loved her—loved her, yet worshiped Dolores as his gods. Letting the ax fall to his elbow by the thong at the haft, he stooped and tenderly picked up the girl, carrying her as a child carries a doll; yet his face was averted from Pascherette's passionate lips that sought to kiss him.

"Not yet can I forgive thee," he said. "Be content that I shall not kill thee, girl. Perhaps, if thy acts have failed in their end, I may forgive thee; not yet."

He carried her around to the great rock, and through the passage into the great chamber, bursting in upon a situation of growing intensity. Dolores sat on a corner of the table, with all her seductive lures in her beautiful face, smiling invitingly at Rupert Venner. Craik Tomlin glared at both, yet his gaze seemed hard to restrain from wandering around the gorgeous chamber, whose wealth he saw now for the first time. Venner, too, had been seized by the jewel-hunger, although neither he, nor Tomlin, guessed at the immensely greater wealth that had been revealed to Pearse. As for Pearse, he sat glowering in his chair, nervous and smoldering; ready at a hint to draw steel without caring what the object. He simply saw rivalry where fifteen minutes before he had thought his own course clear.

Milo appeared to them; carrying his sobbing burden, and the interruption brought a blaze of fury to Dolores's face. She went pale, and her hands clenched and opened nervously.

"Well, slave?" she cried, and Milo started. Never had she used that tone to him.

"Sultana, I thought thou wert alone," he replied, haltingly. "I have brought Pascherette to thee for forgiveness."

"I forgive? Pish! What care I for thy chit? Take her where ye will, and trouble me not with such trash. Out, now! Let me not see her face again, and I care not what ye do with her. But haste. I have work for thee and a score of slaves. Bring them here quickly!"

Silently Milo bore Pascherette to the small room beyond the great chamber, which had been her resting-place while not in attendance on Dolores. And there, still shaking his head to her plea, though with deepening trouble in his eyes, he left her, crying herself into a fitful slumber.

Then with slaves dragged from the corners where they had cowered during the fight, he entered the great chamber, and at Dolores's command set them to carrying out the closed treasure-chests that stood in their old places around the walls.

And the sight of the great chests actually going out brought fiery jealousy back to the eyes of the three yachtsmen. Now Dolores half-closed her own inscrutable eyes, and watched them, catlike, cunning. Pearse sprang from the great chair and began pacing the floor in a heat. Venner aloneseemed to retain any vestige of control over his feelings; and he rapidly lost his color and began to peer about him.

One chest went out, and the cries of the slaves could be heard as they lowered it over the cliff. They returned for another, and now Dolores leaped to her feet and followed them, flinging over her shoulder a smile of invitation. Pearse answered instantly; the others paused. Then she laughed like a siren and held out her hands to the hesitant ones, and said softly and pleasantly:

"Have no fears, timid ones. Thy minds are indeed hard to fathom. I but want to show thee how I am repaying thee for thy sufferings here. Come."

They followed her, and together they entered the rocky tunnel. At the end of it the yellow sunlight blazed like a fire, in the circular aperture was framed a picture of wonderful beauty. The blue sky, flecked with fleecy cloudlets, filled the upper half of the circle; then the sparkling sea of deeper blue lifted its dazzling whitecaps to the kiss of the trades and formed a gem-like background for the brazen sands, the glowing green-and-purple of the Point, and the dainty ivory-and-gold of the white schooner.

It was all mellowed and diminished as seen through a glass at great distance; and on the shore the men toiling to load a great treasure-chest into a long-boat looked like tiny manikins posed about a delicate model of marine life. The second chest yet stood on the cliff-edge, slaves about it lashing double slings and tackles that led from a boulder for lowering it down.

Dolores stepped back, permitting the three men to take in the view without restriction. And she watched them again, her face enigmatic if they glanced at her, breaking into an expression of nearing triumph when they looked away, and left her free to scrutinize them. She saw John Pearse step a pace behind the others, and his fingers clutched absently at his rapier-hilt while the veins on his neck stood out and throbbed like live things.

"One more chest, perhaps two, and I shall see who will be my man!" she whispered to herself.

Then she left them without a word, and returned to the great chamber, where she snatched up an immense rope of pearls and resumed her seat on the edge of the table. There she sat, giving them no glance, when the three men came back, hastily, uneasily, one behind the other, with Tomlin bringing up the rear, scowling at Venner's back malevolently.

Idly now Dolores rolled her pearls on the table, and one by one she crushed them with her dagger-hilt—crushed in one moment the wealth of many a petty princeling, and still crushed gem after gem without so much as a flicker of interest on her cool face. The three men glared at her, and at each other, and the stress they were under could be felt like an impending electric storm. Tomlin's teeth gritted together harshly, his lips were dripping saliva, and he could stand it no longer. He stepped suddenly before Dolores, seized her hands, and cried:

"Woman, you are mad! Do you know what those things are? They are pearls, woman, pearls! Stop this crazy destruction, and in God's name let us go before you madden us."

Dolores turned her cool gaze upon him, drew her hand away easily yet without apparent effort, and crushed another pearl between her gleaming teeth.

"Pearls?" she repeated, tossing away the shattered gem. "Pearls, yes, friend. What of it? Do ye value these trifles, then? Pish! I have such things as these, aye, one for every hair on thy hot head. But let ye go—ha! That is in thy hands, my friend, thine and thy companions."

"Yes, we know your price!" gasped Venner hoarsely, staring full into her eyes. "But what is to prevent us now, when we have you alone, and that great giant is away, from binding you fast and sailing away with the treasure you have already put in my vessel?"

"What can prevent?" she echoed, simulating surprise that such a question should occur to any one. "Nothing shall prevent, my friend, if any of ye think to try it. Have I not said my treasure is for the man who wins it. Am I not waiting for the man able to take it, that I may go with him, too?Here—" She suddenly flung down the pearls at Tomlin's feet, glided close to Venner, and thrust her red lips up to him, her violet eyes like brimming pools behind her drooping lashes. "Here, tie me, my Rupert. Here are my hands; there my feet. Bind me well, and go if thou canst. What, wilt thou not? There, I knew thee better than thou knowest thyself."

She stepped back with a low laugh, and her arm brushed his cheek, sending the hot blood surging to his temples. John Pearse crouched toward Venner, as if waiting for him to lay a finger on Dolores at his peril. She smiled at all three, and stepped over to the side of the chamber, where she carelessly pointed out sacred vessels and altar furnishings, gems of art and jewel-crusted lamps.

"Here, also, is a reason why ye will not go, my friends. Your eyes, accustomed to these things in the great world outside, dare not ignore their worth. And I tell ye that all the treasure now going to the vessel could not purchase the thousandth part of my real treasure, which I will not show, until I know my man." She glanced at Pearse as she spoke, and saw rising greed in his eyes. He had seen the real treasure; he was ripe for her hand. Milo and his slaves returned for another chest, and Dolores waited until they had gone; then she glided swiftly toward the passage, and turned at the door.

"I shall return in fifteen minutes, gentlemen," she said. "Then my man must be ready, or I will drop the great rock at the entrance, and leave ye all three caged here until ye die. For go I will, mated or mateless, with all my treasure, ere the sun sinks into the western sea." And as she left them she flashed a look of appeal at John Pearse.

116

CHAPTER XXI.

THE SLUMBERING SAVAGE.

Pearse followed her with his eyes until she vanished into the passage; then with muttering lips and harshly working features he strode down the chamber to the great tapestry behind which lay the powder store. The suspicion had come to him that Dolores was fooling them all regarding her real treasure; for he believed she had shown him everything, and if those heavy chests contained but a tithe of the whole, life was certain that the gems around the walls were not what she meant when she said she had still a thousand times greater riches than the chests contained.

He tore aside the tapestry, and tried to see through the gloom of the cavern. His eyes could not pierce the blackness, and he looked around for a light, while Venner and Tomlin walked toward him with sudden interest in their faces. Over the tall Hele clock a lantern hung; a gaudy thing of beaten gold, in which an oil wick burned, gleaming out in multicolored light through openings glazed with turquoise and sapphire, ruby, and emerald. He took this down, and impatiently tore away the side of it to secure a stronger light. Again he went to the powder store, and now Venner and Tomlin were at his back, peering over his shoulder or under his arms in curiosity as to his quest.

And, sensing their presence, he swung around upon them savagely, muffling the cry that answered the message of his eyes. Flinging the lantern down, he trampled it out, and with snarling teeth he faced them, his rapier flickering from the sheath like a dart of lightning.

"Back!" he barked, and advanced one foot, falling into a guard. "This is no concern of yours, Venner, nor yours, Tomlin. Back, I say!"

Tomlin stared into his furious face and laughed greedily. His keen eyes had seen a vague, shadowy something in the cavern, that filled him with the same passion which consumed Pearse.

"So you are the lucky one, eh, Pearse?" he chuckled, and his hand went to his own rapier. He stepped back a pace, and, never taking his eyes from Pearse, cried: "Venner, it's you and me against the devil and Pearse! A pretty plot to fool us, indeed; but Pearse was too eager. Peep into that hole, man, and see!"

Venner glared from one to the other, not yet inflamed as they were. But what he saw in their faces convinced him that greatstakes were up to be played for, and he edged forward bent upon seeing for himself.

"Back!" screamed Pearse, presenting his rapier at Venner's breast. Venner persisted, and the steel pricked him. Then, as Tomlin's weapon rasped out, Venner's blood leaped to fighting-heat with his slight wound, and in the next instant the three-sided duel was hotly in progress.

Three-sided it became after the first exchanges. For Pearse, the most skilled in fence, applied himself to Venner as his most dangerous foe, and with the cunning of the serpent Craik Tomlin saw and seized his own opportunity. Let Pearse and Venner kill each other, or let that end be accomplished with his outside help, and there was the solution that Dolores had demanded them to work out; one of them left, to be master of the wealth of Crœsus; to be the mate of a magnificent creature, who could be goddess or she-devil at will.

With a satanic chuckle Tomlin drew back, leaving his friends to fight themselves weary, his own rapier ever presented toward them, urging them on with lashing tongue. And Venner flashed a look at him as Cæsar did at Brutus, and suffered for his lapse in vigilance. For with the pounce of a leopard Pearse was upon him, and his rapier grated over Venner's guard and darted straight at his throat. But Venner's time had not come yet; Tomlin flashed his own weapon in and parried the stroke for him, backing away again with a murderous snarl.

"Not yet, my friends!" he cried. "You're too strong yet, Pearse. At him, Venner; let me see you draw blood as he has, that I may see my own way clearer."

From the other end of the great chamber Dolores watched the conflict from the concealment of the velvet hangings over the door; and her hands were clasped in ecstasy, her lips parted to the swift breathing that agitated her breast; in her blazing eyes her wicked soul lurked, sending out its evil aura to envelop the combatants and instil deeper hatred into them.

The fight raged back and forth around the powder store; once a sudden onslaught by Pearse forced Venner back to the great chair; Tomlin's swift rush to keep close brought all three into a tumbled crash at the dais, and the chair was overturned in a heap of flying draperies that entangled their feet. And while Pearse and Venner struggled vainly to maintain their footing, Tomlin began to accomplish his own dire ends. Crouching, with his dark face full of evil passions, he drove his point first at one, then at the other, stabbing through the involved silk and skins.

In his furious haste to complete his murderous work, he sprang forward carelessly, his foot became entangled, and he pitched face downward upon his victims. Now Pearse seized the opening; but when he arose, stumblingly, there was a different expression on his face, a horror-stricken realization of Tomlin's treachery. Venner lay, still unable to disentangle himself, but slightly hurt, and he, too, regarded Tomlin with a look of sorrow and reawakening sanity.

"Up, murderer, and fight!" rasped Pearse, stepping astride Venner and glaring down at Tomlin. "Venner, draw aside. Let me punish this scoundrel we have called friend; then meet me if you wish."

Tomlin looked up with a snarl of baffled rage, expecting swift reprisal for his treacherous attempt. Gone was the last vestige of civilization from his face; greed of gold, jewel-hunger, blood-lust, all played about his reddened eyes and cruel, down-drawn mouth. The primitive came through the veneer of culture and showed him the man he really was. And evil though his spirit had proved, in this final test his courage showed up like that of the tiger. He leaned on one elbow, watching Pearse like a cat, then slowly knelt and stood, keeping his point down. With the bestial cunning that had overwhelmed him, he circled away from the trappings and draperies of the chair that had brought him down, and responded to Pearse's chivalrous waiting with a sneer.

"You had better have made sure while you had the chance, Pearse," he grinned, showing his teeth wolfishly. "Venner can wait. There is no treasure for three; Dolores is mine! Guard!"

With the word Tomlin made a savage attack without waiting for Pearse to fall into guard. And Dolores came from her concealment, advanced half-way down thechamber, and watched with a new intensity that was not apparent while Venner was in the fight.

Pearse avoided his opponent's thrust at the expense of a pierced left hand, which caught the other's point a hand-breadth from his breast. Then the duel dropped to equality. Swift and silent they fought, silent save for the rasp and screech of steel on steel, their feet padding noiselessly on the deep-piled carpet. Venner drew aside and watched, his eyes losing their hard glare, and some of his old expression returned to his face. It was as if his resurging emotions were bringing back to him the shame and remorse of a gentleman inveigled into performing a despicable action. He, too, saw Dolores approaching; saw the tensity of her expression; sensed some of the tremendous hopes that actuated her, now that she saw the rapid culmination of all her plots and seductions.

She stood quite near to him now, leaning forward in an attitude of utter anxiety. She saw nothing of Venner; her great, violet eyes were dusky and full of yearning, her hands clutched at her breast. And all the intensity of her gaze was fixed upon Tomlin. She responded to his momentary success when he drove Pearse back with a savage assault, with a panting little cry of joy; she fell back with widened eyes when a counter-attack forced Tomlin almost upon her. And her lips opened in a gasp when a vicious clash of steel told of a pressed onslaught, and Pearse lunged heavily forward.

In the instant when Pearse followed his first plunge, Dolores stood in uncertainty through which dawned jubilation. Then her face went white, she seemed to lose all her splendid vitality; for her astounded eyes fastened upon Pearse's rapier-point, protruding a foot from Tomlin's back, and slowly the stricken man sagged away and fell at her feet, clutching at the steel at his breast and snarling like a beast.

A hush fell over the great chamber. Then from a distance came the sound of voices, voices of men down at the shore, ringing clear and sharp on the still air, accentuating the deathly hush that clung around the actors in the scene like a heavy mantle. It startled Dolores into renewed life. She ran with feverish eagerness toward Tomlin, hurling aside the others, and crouching upon the body in dry-eyed rage.

Venner sought to catch the eye of the victor, and saw in Pearse a reflection of the feelings that had possessed himself. John Pearse showed every sign of horror and awakened sanity that had marked his own expression before the fatal fight had started. Their eyes met, and there was no challenge in them. Both dropped their gaze involuntarily upon the huddled figures at their feet; and it was Pearse, the man who had precipitated the conflict at first, who nodded with his head a silent invitation to withdraw. Venner stepped after him, softly and with bowed shoulders, shuddering violently as he passed the expiring Tomlin.

They reached the door together, and with the rocky tunnel open before them, once more holding up to their eyes the picture of absolute beauty of sea and sky and shore, they filled their lungs with fresh, wholesome air, and shook off the last of the evil spell that had held them.

"In God's name, Pearse, let us fly from this hellish place!" whispered Venner, dropping his rapier to the rocky floor with a clatter, and thrusting his hand out in reconciliation.

"Yes, Venner, and pray Heaven we may forget!" replied Pearse fervently. "But how shall we get away? The giant and his crew are yet at the schooner."

"We must wait. They will return soon for more booty. Then we must seize the chance. Is that somebody coming now?"

Milo's great shoulders reared above the cliff, and behind him came the slaves. They came directly toward the great rock, and Pearse flattened himself against the wall in the shadow of the portals, pressing Venner back also with a hand across his chest.

"Hush! Hide here. Let them enter, and we'll make one leap for the shore."

The giant swung into the passage, his black eyes blazing with some emotion that the hidden pair could not fathom. It was something on the border of fear, but of what? Fear and Milo was a combination hard of reconciliation. The slaves at his heels followed dumbly, slaves in thought and action; if their dulled brains everawoke, it was but to the call of animal appetites; they were incapable of devotion such as Milo's, and as incapable of shock should their obedience fail reward. They passed into the great chamber, and a throaty cry of alarm burst from the giant at the sight of his Sultana prone on the floor.

"Now!" whispered Pearse, taking the lead. "Swift and silent!"

Like ghosts they ran from the tunnel, glanced around once as they reached the cliff path, then leaped down the declivity. That swift glance showed them the camp deserted except for the wondering women, who wandered idly among the empty huts, ever looking toward the forest wherein had vanished all their men, waiting with bovine patience for any one to settle their uncertainty for them.

And the forest was yet very still. The Feu Follette lay at a single anchor, heading in the light breeze fair to seaward; a few heads showed above her rail, and the stops had been cast off from her snowy sails. At her gangway a single boat lay, the painter made fast on deck; on the foreshore the other two long-boats were drawn up on the sand, planks running up to their sides in readiness for the embarkation of yet more treasure.

Venner and Pearse raced down the steep path, using little precaution, sending showers of stones and clods flying before them. And Peters, the schooner's sailing-master, saw them coming, and his voice rang out calling for hands to man the boat. Two men answered and entered the boat as the two fugitives reached the shore and ran along the Point. Pearse counted the minutes at their disposal, and saw the futility of waiting for that boat. He clutched eagerly at Venner's arm, and panted in his ear:

"Tell them to hold on! Let them get the schooner ready for swift departure. Come, we must swim for it."

Venner hesitated but a second. Then his hail went hurtling over the still haven, and the two seamen scrambled out of the boat again.

"Swim it is, Pearse," he said, leading the way down to deep water. "Swim it is, and may the ever-cleansing sea wash out of us the last traces of insanity."

Together they plunged into the blue sea and swam swiftly out to the schooner.

CHAPTER XXII.

THE FLIGHT OF THE FEU FOLLETTE.

Dolores, flinging herself down upon Craik Tomlin, seized his face between her hands and raised his head, placing her knee beneath it. She panted like an exhausted doe, yet the fire that leaped from her eyes gave the lie to her attitude of sorrowing humility. Her lips moved feverishly, but she could not or would not speak aloud. Tomlin's eyes were closed in agony, his teeth were clenched tightly upon his under lip; he gave no sign that he knew of her presence. And a sudden fury seized her at his irresponsiveness. She shook his head between her hands savagely.

"Wake! Speak!" she cried hoarsely. "Art indeed dead, at the moment of my triumph?"

Tomlin's eyelids flickered, and his lips strove to speak. One hand went weakly to his face, to grasp her fingers. And into her anxious ear he managed to whisper:

"Evil luck fought with me, Dolores. Yet I die content if you care."

"Care!" she echoed, shaking his fingers loose impatiently. "Care? Yes, this I care, bungler: I care because of all three of thee, thou alone wert covetous enough to obey my conditions. With thee alive, there was hope of thy friends' speedy death. With thee dead, which of the others will wipe his fellow from his path for me? Why, think ye, did I fawn on John Pearse? But to arouse in thee the demon of jealousy; why did I smile on Venner, and call him my Rupert? To steel thy arm against him. And for what?"

She suddenly laid his head down on the floor, leaned over him with her lips almost brushing his cheek, and whispered fiercely: "Speak! Canst live?"

Tomlin's face lost some of its pain. The thin lips straightened into the semblance of a faint smile. His glazing eyes opened slightly.

"I am done for," he whispered. "Dolores, kiss me again. I die for you."

The beautiful fury sprang to her feet, spurning him. She glared down at his chalky face in utter scorn.

"Kiss thee? Thou die for me? Pah! I kiss no carrion. A half-hundred men have died for me this day, I hope. I kiss him who lives for me and conquers, not the weakling who dies!"

Without deigning another glance at her victim, she turned away and went to meet Milo. He now entered with his slaves.

"Where are the two strangers?" she demanded harshly.

Milo returned her stare with a look of simple surprise. He had seen nothing of them, and had thought of them being yet with his mistress.

"I saw them not, Sultana," he replied.

"Saw them not, great clod!" she blazed at him, clenching her hands in rage. "Are they here, then?"

Milo looked around in bewilderment. In all her life Dolores had been his especial care; in her many moments of temper she had perhaps pained his devoted heart, but never had she used to him the tone she now used. It seemed to his simple soul that the foundations of his faith were being wrenched loose.

"I will find them, Sultana," he said quietly, and turned to leave by the tunnel.

"Stay here, thou blind fool!" she commanded him. "I will find them myself. Here is work more fitting for a slave. How many chests are going to the ship?"

"Three."

"And how many have ye yet empty here?"

"Three, lady."

"Then get them quickly. Until I return, bid thy fellows replace the treasure that is still in the powder store. And haste, for I will leave this place this day, though all the fiends say no."

She ran along the tunnel, and Milo set his men to their task. As he passed along to the powder chamber, a low moan arrested him, and he halted in sudden remorse for Pascherette, whom he now felt he had judged harshly. He left his fellows and went to the tiny alcove where the little octoroon lay, and his great heart leaped in response to the worship that shone in her dark eyes. He saw the dry and cracked lips, the flushed face, and fetched water and wine before he would speak to her. Then, with her small head and slender shoulders against his immense chest, he gave her drink, soothing her pain with soft speech and caressing hand.

Pascherette's wound was deep, and bleeding internally; a fever already burned in the tiny maid's veins. She peered up at him wistfully, all of her mischief, all her piquancy gone and replaced by a softened, humbled expression that wrung Milo's heart-strings.

"Will ye not kiss me now, Milo?" she whispered, with a pearly drop brimming from each eye, where laughter had so lately dwelt.

"Pascherette, thy fault was great," he answered, yet in his face was a look so forgiving, so excusing, that the girl shivered expectantly and closed her eyes with a happy sigh.

Yet the kiss was not given. From the great chamber the angry voice of Dolores rang out.

"Milo! Where art thou, slave!"

And the giant tenderly laid Pascherette down again, and ran in answer.

"Sultana?"

"Blind, idle dolt! While thou art fondling that serpent of thine, thy mistress's affairs may go hang! Haste with the treasure, or feel my anger. While thy useless eyes were mooning on nothing, the strangers have escaped. They are even now getting sail on the white vessel. Carry the chests down to the Point as soon as ye may. I will stay them yet, and they shall learn the cost of flouting Dolores! Hasten, I tell ye!"

Milo winced at her address; his black eyes, usually holding the utter devotion of a noble dog, glittered with tiny sparks of resentment; yet the habit of years could not be lightly cast off, and he bowed low, even while Dolores had turned her back on him, and picked up a great empty chest to carry it to the powder store. Here in the flickering light of a pine splinter the slaves worked feverishly, their abject eyes sparkling with borrowed radiance from the riches they handled.

And while they worked, Dolores emerged from the tunnel, flashed one long glance of derision at the moving schooner, and sped down the cliff to stop her flight.

The Feu Follette was poorly enough manned with Peters and his four men. With the ready help of Venner and Pearse the getting of the anchor and the hoisting of the heavy fore and main sails was an arduous job, but it was accomplished under the tremendous urge of remembrance. None wished to have the experiences of the past days repeated; Peters was anxious to get his beautiful vessel into safer waters; the Feu Follette's owner and his guest were doubly anxious to drop those blue hills of ominous memory below the horizon forever. They gave scant attention to the three great iron-bound chests that stood between the guns along the waist; getting clear occupied every faculty.

The tide setting directly on the Point, with a breeze dead in from seaward, forced the schooner perilously close to the bar that had been her undoing before; but, with the lead going, Peters speedily found that his previous mishap must undoubtedly have been due to clever misleading. After touching lightly once, and getting deeper water at the next cast over the lee side, he understood the trick of the extended false Point and stood boldly along shore.

And as the schooner gathered steerage-way, hugging the Point closely, Dolores ran out along the sandy beach and plunged into the sea abreast the moving vessel.

"Here's that vixen woman, sir!" cried Peters angrily, looking toward Venner for instructions. Peters had the helm, and owner and guest stood against the companion, ready to lend a hand at the sheets, forward or aft.

Venner and Pearse stared at the swimmer, then turned and gazed searchingly at each other. In the face of each lingered a trace of the subjection they had fallen under; neither could quite so quickly forget the allurements of this woman. Her kisses had been as sweet as her fury had been terrible; and the absence of Craik Tomlin was an additional incentive to memory.

"Shall we take her away?" asked Venner, avoiding Pearse's eye as he put the question.

"Can't you make more sail, Peters?" was Pearse's reply.

Venner laughed softly, agreeably; and the next moment Dolores hailed them. She swam swiftly, with effortless ease, slipping through the sea like a sparkling nymph in her native element. But the schooner traveled fast, and, though she lost no ground, she gained but slowly. She hailed again.

"Rupert, my Rupert!" and finished the cry with a rippling laugh. "Art stealing my treasure and leaving me?"

"By Heavens, Pearse, I had forgotten these chests," said Venner uneasily. Pearse regarded him closely, fearing that Dolores's spell was yet powerful. He gripped Venner tightly by the arm, leaned nearer, and said:

"Venner, so long as that blood-polluted treasure is on your deck, so long will you be unable to settle your mind. Bid the hands pitch it into the sea, for God's sake!"

A lull in the wind slowed the schooner down, and Dolores gained a fathom. Her fair face was set toward them in a bewitching smile, and she waved a gleaming arm at them. Venner fought with himself in silence for a brief while, then with a shudder stepped to the wheel.

"Get the hands, Peters," he told the sailing-master, "and heave those chests overboard. Quickly! You shall lose nothing by this, but don't delay a moment!"

126

CHAPTER XXIII.

STUMPY FIRES THE MAGAZINE.

Milo and his slaves worked frenziedly at their task, his suddenly bitter spirit flogging them to unremitting haste. In the giant's troubled face the smoldering spark of resentment had grown to an incipient blaze that required but a breath to burst into angry flame.

One great chest was filled with the choicest of the gems in the powder store; it was set aside in the entrance beside the tapestry, and another box was opened before the powder-kegs. Little Pascherette had ceased moaning, but from time to timea choking sob sounded from her alcove that increased the hard brilliancy of the light in Milo's eyes. The great chamber was silent as a mausoleum in the intervals between the clashing and tinkling of gold and stones in the chest; from the outside, by way of the rock tunnel, came only the sigh and murmur of the crooning breeze, the softened plash of the tide on the shore, the scream of wheeling seabirds. All sound of the schooner had departed; there was no human note in the whole region.

Then, as the second chest was almost full, and Milo pulled the third and last along in readiness, from the secret gallery behind the Grove came the shouts and oaths of men, weary, footsore men, but men with animal appetites whetted by the day of bloody conflict. They could be heard at the great door in the painting of the "Sleeping Venus"; not knowing its secret their way was barred. But Stumpy's hoarse roar could be heard calling them back to the ledge, and there was a note of menace in his tired tones. And mingling with his voice was the voice of a woman of the camp, raised in shrill complaint. Milo stepped to the picture and listened.

"I tell ye the fiend has tricked ye, Stumpy!" the woman cried.

"Tricked me? Have a care how ye talk that way, woman!" Stumpy's voice replied warningly.

"Aye, tricked ye and me and all of us! Even now—come to the cliff, and I'll show ye."

The scrambling of heavy feet could be heard in the gallery as men rushed out in answer. How many men Milo could not determine; but fewer than had followed Stumpy into the forest in chase of their broken foes. The slaves at the treasure-chests paused in their work, alarm on their shining faces, looking ever toward Milo for instructions.

Milo ran back through the great chamber and out by the tunnel to the cliff, peering around for Stumpy and hoping to see the schooner putting back.

Without Dolores he was at a loss; yet he was not ready to leave his charge to be gazed upon by untried eyes. His breast swelled nigh to bursting at sight of the schooner. The Feu Follette was but half a mile away in a straight line from the cliff; she had been tacking against a light breeze and flood tide around the Point, and while she had sailed several miles through the water, she had but just gained past the face of the cliff. And far from returning, she sailed farther and farther away as he watched, nursed with such skill of sheet and helm as proved to Milo's seamanly eye that her people would never return of their free will. And what of Dolores? His condor's vision picked her out as soon as the schooner. Her gleaming arms and shoulders swept rhythmically over and over, cleaving the sea easily and smoothly, her lustrous hair streaming behind her, and the sun glinting brightly from the gold circlet around her head. She was gaining foot by foot, and Milo keenly scrutinized the schooner for signs of surrender. There were none. At the schooner's rail three heads were visible; but Milo knew neither belonged to Venner nor Pearse. That persuaded him that the schooner was unlikely to come back. And the even, tireless manner in which Dolores swam convinced him that she would follow to the end. Yet he would not utterly believe she had deserted him. He glared around for the men whose voices he heard now, raised in anger in chorus with the voices of the woman and her companions. Stumpy stepped out from the grove path with but four men behind him; and they were in sore plight. Stumpy himself dangled an idly swinging sleeve that was stained dark-red to the shoulder. A red sear across his nose and cheek rendered him a demoniacal figure through the powder, smoke and sweat. And his mates were tattered and cut, their shirts bore red splashes to a man; their grimed faces and fiery eyes held the passions of blooded men who see their reward flying from them.

"I tell ye she's gone for good!" cried the woman who had brought the news to Stumpy. "See, she's almost there, and three chests of treasure have gone in that vessel! Her swimming after it is but a part of her cuteness. Now d'ye believe, fools!"

The crippled, battle-scarred pirate glared to seaward with red-rimmed eyes in which flames of revenge started into life. Histwisted, warped life had been spent in fighting and trickery; to-day his work had culminated in a brave stand for what

128

he thought to be straight and right; reward he expected, but he had earned it with blood and sweat, hoping at the last that some of his earlier transgressions might be atoned for in his loyalty to his mistress.

He hurled aside the persistent women, who sought some reassuring word from him, and mouthing rather than speaking a call to his men to follow, he plunged again into the grove path and stumbled toward the ledge entrance. Here he clambered painfully to the gallery, cursing to himself bitterly, never looking back to see if his men followed, intent only upon one absorbing thing. Revenge was beyond him, since there were left no subjects for his revenge. He had never seen the great stone at the chamber portals left rolled aside; could not even now imagine such a situation. No, if Dolores were gone in truth, and with her the strangers and the treasure, then it was certain, he thought, that the great chamber was sealed forever. And he would see into its mysteries, even though they proved barren now. He knew the way; Dolores had shown him.

Feverishly hunting for a flint, he tore some threads from his shirt and frayed them into tow. Then with his cutlas he struck a spark and ignited his threads, carefully nursing the tiny flame until he could find a dry stick. This lasted him until a pine torch was found, and then he crawled along the gallery in search of the powder train. That, he knew, for she had told him, would burst the rock asunder anyhow; and that would be enough, for he had guessed shrewdly that the gallery was connected with the great chamber by some secret egress.

And who knew? Might not Dolores have taken in her haste but part of her vast store? Stumpy knew as well as Red Jabez the tremendous wealth that had been deposited in that chamber of mysteries; for he had been with the red chief from the beginning; he had seen with his own eyes the riches of a hundred ships taken in there, and never a thing come out.

"She can't have bagged the lot," he muttered, fanning his torch into a red flare. "But she'll pay for deserting Stumpy, or Stumpy's a liar!"

He found the powder train, and the moisture had dried from it, leaving only a little line of dry, quick-igniting powder. He was not sure just where the magazine was; not sure how long the train would burn before the explosion. So down he clambered again, searching at the great altar for the water-vessels he knew should be there. Then, with a jar of water, he returned to his train, and swiftly swept up the dry powder and moistened it a little, making a rough slow match of it.

"Now we'll see the sights!" he growled, and went to the end of the gallery and flung his torch into the train.

He watched it for a moment, to be sure that it would burn, then stepped down from the ledge and drew back a safe distance to watch the upheaval. To what extent the mine was intended to destroy he had no idea. He simply knew that Dolores had pointed it out to him as a means of defense should the gallery be carried in the attack. He supposed, therefore, that it would shatter the gallery. Doing that, it must surely dislodge or loosen rock enough for him to break into the great chamber with aid.

The thought recalled his men to his mind, and he saw for the first time that they had not followed him. He started down the path toward the camp, shouting to them by name, eager to give them an inkling of the treat in store. But his hail was answered by another, and down the path a woman appeared running, her hair flying, and tremendous excitement in every line of her face.

"Stumpy! Stumpy!" she sobbed and cried in hysterical intoxication. "Oh, Stumpy, the great chamber is open, and it's full of gold and treasure!"

CHAPTER XXIV.

MILO CROSSES THE BAR.

Milo watched Stumpy disappear down the grove path, and heard him call to his men to follow. Then he regarded the receding yacht intently for amoment, and the last vestige of noble devotion went from his face and gave place to a great and absorbing bitterness. In that instant, the foundations, pillars, and capitals of his soul shook and tottered; his universe changed from a thing of golden beauty and heavenly splendor to a shameful mockery of truth and faith.

In that moment his thoughts flew back to little Pascherette, and his great heart yearned toward her. False she had proved, but to what? To whom? He asked himself these things as he slowly walked back along the tunnel, not yet knowing what he would do. He answered his own question. Pascherette had proven false to falsity; she had schemed against the schemer; and, in the other tray of the balance she had done these things for love of him, out of a deep and all-powerful ambition to place him, Milo the slave, in the high place of the wanton ingrate who had deserted her people. And the thought hurt him now; he had not yet yielded her the kiss she craved. Even now the little gold-tinted one might be cold in death, denied that small consolation because of his obstinate heart.

He ran along the tunnel and burst through the great chamber, cursing the idle slaves into silence when they cried their helpless queries at him. And straight to Pascherette he sped, to fling himself down by her side and seize her tiny, moist hand in frantic appeal.

"Pascherette!" he whispered with a dry sob. "Little golden one, speak to thy Milo. Speak, and forgive!"

The octoroon gave no sign of life, and the giant dropped her hand and gently raised her pallid face. His lips sought hers in a passionate kiss, long and yearning; and slowly her eyelids fluttered and opened. The dark eyes were misty, yet that longed-for kiss had brought back her fleeting spirit to recognize her man. She closed her tired eyes again, with a little sign, and the small, pale lips formed the words: "I am content, Milo, my god."

The giant bowed his head over her silent face, and his black eyes searched for a returning flicker of vitality. It was gone forever. Pascherette was dead; and Milo laid her head down gently, and drew back to stare at her with growing rebellion and horror. What gods could there be to use him thus? He leaped to his feet with arms flung upward.

"Hah, gods of earth and sea, witness Milo's penitence!" he said hoarsely. "To Dolores I have given the worship that belonged to ye and ye have taken terrible atonement. Pity me!"

He paced the small alcove nervously, seeking light where no light was. Then the harsh shouts of Stumpy's men resounded through the chamber, and he stepped outside in alarm. For it was not yet possible for him to discard the usage of years which forbade intrusion in that secret place. He saw Stumpy's four men standing open-mouthed in the doorway beneath the yellow lantern, gazing ludicrously at the magnificence of the furnishings. The slaves at the powder store stood where he had left them, idle and aimless, but with an open chest at their feet. This now attracted the pirates' attention, and with a stamp and a shout they roared through the great chamber, their faces awork with newly aroused avarice.

Just for one second Milo pondered staying them. But his soul had soured; he uttered a grunt of scornful disgust, and waved a hand at them, muttering:

"Revel, ye dogs! Plunge thy hands deep. 'Tis all thine, and the fiend's blessing go with it!"

He returned to his dead Pascherette and knelt beside her, patting her cold hands and speaking to her softly and tenderly. Out in the chamber the pirates had hurled aside the slaves, and, flinging open the chests, were glaring with wolfish eyes and dripping jaws at the bewildering mass of treasure revealed.

Their noise irritated Milo. He went out again to stop them. And he saw a pirate snatch up a glittering tiara and place it on his head with a roaring oath. He saw another snatch the bauble off; and in a breath the pirates were at each other's throats; cutlases flashed and a savage fight began at the moment the women stole in to see the mysterious place, and one of their number ran to bring Stumpy.

The giant glowered at the snarling menas at some repulsive beasts, horrified that they should thus desecrate the quiet of his Pascherette's death-bed. He was not the Milo of old now. His memory had flown back through the years to the time when he was a youth of position and great promise in his own land; when, instead of being the cast-off servant of a beautiful ingrate, he numbered his own servants by hundreds. And a great dignity stole into his ennobled face. He softly picked up the dead girl, and advanced toward the rock tunnel.

Stumpy met him at the door, and the crippled pirate's eyes burned with the new-born lust of loot. Stumpy made as if to stay the giant with questions; but he saw the snarling fight at the end of the chamber and caught the glitter of jewels. With the stumbling speed of a charging, wounded bull, he rushed in to join battle.

Running women brushed against Milo in the passage; all the camp's living people had caught the fever. The giant strode on, until he stood in the rugged rock portals and gazed once more over the sea. The schooner had moved but slightly since he last looked at her; he could see Dolores's head still advancing, and very near to the vessel now. The breeze had lulled, perhaps preceding a shift of wind; and the visible people on the deck of the Feu Follette appeared to be running back and forth in indecision.

At Milo's right hand the great rock sat on its ledge, ready to fall at a touch, and his brooding eyes flashed to it with terrible meaning. Inside, the great chamber resounded with the clash of steel, the shouts of furious human beasts, and the shrill cries of women urging them on; for there must be victors, even to such a sordid fight, and to the victors, spoils. Where victors and spoils are, there harpy women await them.

Milo gazed long and passionately into the face of his dead; then he laid her softly down outside the rock and arose with a fierce light irradiating his face.

"Dogs, who would thus break the sleep of my beloved, I give ye good for evil!" he muttered. "Treasure ye crave: treasure I give ye, and none may take it from ye!"

He turned, put his hand upon the great rock and started it from its bed. And as he moved the mass, the mountain rocked and crashed with the thunder of the bursting powder-magazine.

Down came the great rock, pinning Milo beneath it, threatening in its final fall to crush him and the body of his love. His great arms shot out and up, every muscle on his colossal frame stood out like ropes, his back cracked with the tremendous strain. He stiffened his knees, bit into his lip until the blood gushed; and a groan burst from his breast as he felt his stout knees stagger.

His bulging eyes glared ahead over the sea; into the air flew a thousand fragments of shattered rock; they fell and thrashed the sea into foam a mile from shore. Rocks fell upon his already overwhelming burden; his knees bent, and the blood trickled from his nostrils. And with his fast ebbing breath he breathed his valedictory, fixing his stony eyes upon Pascherette as upon his deity.

"Gods of my fathers, receive my spirit into thy halls. Let thy swift justice overtake the cause of this upheaval; and receive with my spirit the spirit of the one who loved me." He fell to one knee, and a great sob shook him. The rock was falling in a shower about him; it rang and crashed on the gigantic stone that was crushing him. He bent his gaze in anguish afresh on the dead girl, now almost buried under stone and earth, and murmured: "Pascherette, I come! I see beyond the blue ocean and the golden horizon the throne of my gods. Come, golden one, let us go. There will our faithfulness meet just reward!"

He pitched forward upon the dead girl, and the great rock crashed down, building them a tomb grand as the eternal hills.

CHAPTER XXV.

THE TOLL OF THE GODS.

Venner's order to heave the treasure-chests overboard was not given without a pang of regret. It was scarcely obeyed without threats; for the sailing master had been bitten by the treasurefever before his owner and guest came on board. Had they not appeared when they did, the schooner had gone without them, and Peters had already seen a golden vista ahead of him. He hesitated now, and Venner left the wheel vacant to urge him.

"Over with it, I say! At once! Here, Pearse, lend a hand here, man, before that witch's great eyes mesmerize us again. See, she smiles yet, and comes nearer."

Reluctantly the seamen raised one iron-bound chest to the rail and poised it there. From the water astern rang Dolores's throaty laugh, even and full breathing, as if she had not swam a fraction of the half-mile she had covered.

"Foolish Rupert!" she cried, never relaxing her stroke. "Why waste the fruits of thy pains? Hast looked inside then? Nay, take me on board, and let us look together. Thou wilt not see Dolores drown, I swear. Then look once more into my eyes, my Rupert!"

She laughed again mockingly, alluringly, and Pearse turned away with a shudder, not daring to cast a glance in the direction of Venner.

"Throw the stuff over, I say!" cried Venner hoarsely, and gave the chest a push that sent it into the rippling sea with a thunderous splash. And again that mocking laugh rang out astern; it was nearer, and Dolores's beautiful face was turned up to them with triumph in every feature. She had seen the struggle going on in her two intended victims; if she could but gain to within whispering distance of either of them, surely she would never let them escape her.

"Come, take me on board, my Rupert. I have a secret to tell thee, but thee alone!" she cried, and spurted swiftly, gaining abreast of the main-chains.

But the eyes of Venner and Pearse were fixed in astonishment upon the tall cliff they had left; their eyes stared amazedly, and they stood like statues, hearing none of her seductive words.

"What do ye see?" she demanded, frowning up at them.

A score of sharp splashes in the water around the schooner startled her. She suspected they were hurling missiles at her, and one struck her arm. She turned swiftly and her face darkened with fury. Then more small objects fell about her, and one struck her arm. She turned swiftly on her side to seek the source, and in her ears boomed the tremendous crash of Stumpy's explosion, rolling far over the sea, reverberating from the shores and making the air quiver like a solid thing.

A great mass of rock hurtled overhead, missed the schooner by scant feet, and Venner shouted in horror:

"Throw her a line, Pearse! Here, quickly, before she is crushed by such a rock as that one!"

The sea was shattered into foam for fathoms around, and every face on the Feu Follette stared over the rail in helpless astonishment. But on the face of Dolores glowed a smile of triumph. She feared nothing of earth or heaven; among the flying rocks she swam on toward the schooner, smiling up at them, waiting for the rope that meant victory to her.

And in the brief space before the rope hurtled out, down from the heavens plunged a high-flung piece of granite fair upon Dolores. She seemed to sense its shadow, and in the moment it struck her she half sank, breaking its force. But it followed her down. The mass struck between her gleaming shoulders, and she flung up her arms in despair, turning over and over with the impact, then floating unconscious close by the side of the white schooner that had been her goal.

"God! Get her aboard!" gasped Pearse. "She's done for. Yet we cannot leave her there for the sharks, like a beast!"

Venner and Peters were already trying with boat-hooks to catch Dolores's tunic. Pearse threw a line over the girl and drew her nearer and the hooks took hold. They drew her up the side with a care that amounted to reverence, for in her unconsciousness she was more beautiful than ever, her fine features molded in dead white, traced with fine blue veins; the grace of her form was that of a lovely sculpture now, lacking vitality, but possessing every line of perfection. The blow that had overtaken her had failed in its terrible threat to crush her.

"Lay her in the companionway on the lounge," said Venner. He ran to the saloon and brought up wine. He bathed her temples and wrists with the liquor, and forced some between her blue lips. And Pearse chafed her hands and patted them, gazing down at her in silent awe.

"Venner," he whispered, when her eyes refused to open, "we must let this settle the score against her. It's a terrible end for such a creature."

"For my part, Pearse, I would give all I have just to see those great violet eyes laugh at me again; to hear that mocking laugh from her maddening lips. God, will she never awake?"

Astern of the schooner the sun was slowly descending to the western sea-rim, and as the course was resumed after picking up Dolores, the Point and the cliff gradually drew out across the path of the sun, until the outlines of the rock and trees stood out black and sharp. On the cliff-top a heavy pall of greasy smoke hung low about the shattered pirates' camp; from fissures high up the frowning side spirals of smoke testified to the wide-spread destruction that followed the blast.

They looked at the terrific devastation, and again at its nearer victim. And as they gazed down at her, Dolores's lips trembled in a faint smile, her great eyes opened wide, looking directly and fearlessly back at them.

"I thank ye, my friends; I knew you would take me," she whispered, and the two men turned away with a shudder. As she had lived, Dolores was now meeting her inevitable end, bold and indomitable.

"Where are you hurt?" inquired Venner lamely. "Let me do something to ease you."

"Ease?" she laughed as of old, but her teeth clenched upon her lower lip immediately, with the pain it caused. "I shall ask ye to ease me presently, good friends. Grim Death has me by the throat already. But carry me outside. I am stifling in here. Let me see the ocean and the sky at least in my passage. And I have something to tell ye also."

On the gratings around the stern, abaft the wheel, they laid her on soft cushions. She drank greedily of the wine and water they offered her; she quivered with eagerness to unburden her mind before her thirst was quenched forever. She motioned them, to bend over her, and began to speak in, husky whispers.

"That chest, thou cast it overboard. Dost know what was in it?"

Both shook their heads. None had seen inside the chests after they came from the great chamber.

"I'll tell ye, then, for the peace of your souls and the tranquillity of your voyage. Lest thy men be seized with a desire for treasure that shall work ye mischief, have them open the other two chests. Quickly, for I am faint."

Venner went to the chests himself and flung back the lids, which were bolted on the outside and not locked. He stared for a moment, unbelievingly, then nodded to Pearse. Pearse stared, too, in amazement, and one after the other the sailors were called to see. They saw two great strong-boxes filled to the brim with iron chains, broken cutlases, rusty bilboes, and rock; a fool's treasure in truth.

"'Twas a trick to set my rascals at odds," Dolores told them when they returned to her. "To thee, Pearse, I showed my treasure, and I fear that blast has buried it beneath a mountain. Milo was to take it out. I cannot believe it can have been taken away ere that powder blew it to fragments. It was still in the powder store."

"Yes, I know," said Pearse quietly. "It was that which precipitated the fight between us three that killed poor Tomlin."

"Well, if thou still art hungry for treasure, my friends, there is my store buried where thou knowest, and I shrewdly fear but few of my people are left. But I am slipping. Stand aside, that I may close my eyes on the place I called home."

Dolores ceased speaking and lay, scarcely stirred by her faint respiration, gazing over the schooner's stern at the sinking sun. The golden disk was turning to red and across its darkened face the cliff and Point stood out in sharp silhouette, which grew larger as the great glowing sun was distorted and enlarged by the refraction near the horizon. The breeze had changed, and now blew with gentle strength out of the west, a fair wind for their homeward course, and the strands of Dolores's glorious hair blew about her face like tendrils about an orchid of unearthly beauty.

Presently she stirred again, and now she summoned all her remaining vitality to raise herself on an elbow. Pearse and Venner leaned closer, sensing the end in the tremendous brilliancy of her wide, dry eyes.

She spoke softly, yet with a thrilling note of yearning that choked her hearers with harsh sobs.

"Father, I come," she whispered. "If I have failed in obeying thy commands, I ask forgiveness, for I am but a woman. A woman with instincts and yearnings, born of the mother I never knew. Thy very treasures that were to appease me put the yearning more strongly in my brain. Thy teachings showed me a world of beasts and savagery; thy treasures gave me dreams of a world peopled by such as I would be. My mother's blood forced me to seek this other, better world; thy blood forced me to seek it wrongfully."

She paused, and gathered her fleeting breath.

Then, sitting suddenly upright, she flung both arms out to the setting sun now lipping the sea, and cried:

"Gods I know not. Yet must there be such, else had I never known the devotion of a Milo! Wherever ye be, brave Milo, living or dead, commend me to thy own gods and forgive me for my ingratitude." She seized Venner and Pearse by the arms as she fell back, and whispered: "In pity, friends, set my feet toward the west, and launch my poor body down the sun path as it sinks into the blue Caribbean that was

138

my only home."

She relaxed with a little shivering sigh, the glorious eyes closed with a tired tremor, and the spirit of Dolores the beautiful, the wicked, the tempestuous, winged its way down the mysterious paths of the dark unknown.

"Come," said Venner, suddenly shaking off his abstraction, "time is all too short if we are to render her this last small service."

"How shall we do it?" asked Pearse doubtfully.

"We shall send her down her chosen path in a boat. Peters will load the dingey with ballast, while you and I will lay Dolores out as well as we may. Bring me that grating, Pearse. We will speed her in the dress she loved. Her soul would sicken at a suffocating winding sheet. Hurry, for the sun is half gone!"

Swiftly they worked, these men who had cause to remember the departed siren without great love, and they placed her, secured to a grating, across the thwarts of the dingey, to which the grating was in turn secured. Then, all prepared, Peters sprang into the boat, bored a score of auger-holes in the bottom, and as the great red sun set fierce and blazing behind the black profile of the cliff, the filling boat was set adrift, straight down the path of the luminary, bound ever westward, until the sea gods claimed it and its passenger for their own.

"Farewell, place of ill-luck!" cried Pearce, as the schooner bore away before the rising evening breeze. "May I never set my eyes on such evil shores again."

"Then you will not come back to seek the treasure?" asked Venner, with a shadowy flicker of a smile.

"Not for a thousand times the treasure that lies there!" cried Pearse vehemently. "And I have seen it! The horror of this will haunt me until my dying day. I only hope God will look kindly upon that poor woman, that's all."

"I hope so, too," rejoined Venner thoughtfully. "With a white woman's opportunities, what a woman she could have been."

But the gods are inscrutable. Only the warm mantle of the setting sun gave a hint that Dolores might be even now entering into a place of eternal rest, where her sins of ignorance and untutored instincts would not count too heavily against her. The sea is very benign to its elect; a calm sea in the setting sun received Dolores in arms of infinite benignity.

THE END